Landon Brary

and

The Land of Nod

by: Joshua Thomas Bray

Welcome to the Dreamdom

Prologue

Prologue:

David hid under his blankets, holding his breath as he desperately tried to stay silent. His thin sheets did nothing to stop him from shaking. Gripping his pillow tightly, he forced himself to keep from crying. His heart raced at the ghostly sound of a door slowly creaking. Heavy footsteps pounded the floor as they moved closer to his bed. David did all he could to stem his shivering. The footsteps ceased and silence shrouded the room. He let out a nervous breath and quickly covered his mouth with both hands. His heart beat hard and rapidly while he stifled his breathing. Utterly terrified, the sheets along with David were viciously yanked to the floor. He tore himself free and scrambled to the wall. Starring wide-eyed, he searched his room; from within the dark corner, directly across from him, came a soft thud.

"Mom!"

Straining his eyes to see in the dark, David searched for any sign of movement. Carefully moving away from the wall, he inched through the room with his hands stretched out until he felt the corner of his desk. He opened the top drawer and quickly found the cool plastic of a red flashlight. He grabbed it and quickly returned his back against the wall. David took in a deep breath and with trembling hands, he flicked the flashlight on and poured the soft yellow ray of light upon the dark corner across his room. It was empty. He poured the light all around his room but found no sign of an intruder. Suddenly, David's door burst open and the blinding light of his ceiling lamp sliced through the darkness.

"What's the matter, honey?" screamed a panicked woman clenching a baseball bat ready to strike.

"There's something in my room!"

David's mother cautiously searched the room, looking behind his door first. Next, under his bed. And finally, the closet. She reached out a single foot, opened the door while holding the baseball bat over her shoulder, ready to swing as she kicked the door open. It was empty, except for his clothes and a few boxes of comics on the floor. She lowered the bat and then pulled him from the wall into her arms as she sat down on his bed.

"Sweetheart, I know you get scared at night," she said softly. "And, I know you miss your Daddy but, we have to be strong. There's nothing in here."

"There was something in here, Mom," David whispered as she wiped the tears from his cheeks.

"I know, sweetheart. I believe you think you saw someone. You've had a rough week and s stressed mind can play tricks on you. Especially, after these past few weeks. Now, you're totally safe and can get back to sweet dreams," she replied, letting loose from her hold and kissing his forehead.

David nodded, pulled his sheets back up from the floor and then slid under his covers. After double checking and reassuring him that there was no one in his room, David's mother turned his on small silver lava lamp, smiled lovingly at him, and turned off the lights.

"Good night, honey. I love you."

"Love you too, Momma,"

As she made her way down the hall, she heard something quickly shuffle behind her. She whipped around, held up the baseball bat, and asked nervously,

"David?"

She cautiously made her way back to her son's door. As she got closer she saw wisps of smoke billowing out from underneath his door. David's mother ran and tried to push the door open, but it was instantly slammed in her face. She desperately twisted the knob back and forth while slamming her shoulder into the door with all her might, slowly breaking the wood that the strike plate was affixed to.

"Mom!" David screamed.

Her heart started to pound as a wave of anxiety washed over and flooded her body. After a few solid hits she burst through the door and was instantly slammed to the floor. There, towering above her stood a large dark figure wrapped in a suffocating cloud of black smoke and ash, two blazing emerald eyes staring menacingly down at her as she struggled to regain her footing.

As the smoke let her loose, David's mother scrambled to the wall. She tried flicking the light switch on, but nothing happened. Peering through the thick smoke, she saw her son dangling in the air, a rotting hand with silver claws violently choking him, cutting into his neck. She watched in horror as his legs kicked and heard the gurgle of him trying to call out to her.

She darted towards her son but was effortlessly slammed back down onto the floor. Smoke and ash swiftly wrapped around her face and started to replace the air in her lungs. With all her might, she pushed her body off the floor and stood up. Coughing and struggling to breathe, David's mother blindly reached out for her son, and staggered through the suffocating smoke

Suddenly, the glass from David's bedroom window exploded and a frozen wind sliced through the room. The smoke thinned and a massive figure clad in dark armor stood in the frame holding David by the throat. Its armor dripped like oil and in between the black metal plates were red-hot glowing embers, searing its flesh. Its eyes blazing wildly as a silver grin full of long sharp teeth began to form a wicked smile. Suddenly, David was carelessly tossed out the window onto the icy grass below. A deep and terrifying laughter roared through the room as the terrifying figured transformed into smoke and poured itself out into the night air.

David's mother ran to the window and saw her son being dragged by his head across the ground and into the darkness. David reached out and screamed to his mother before disappearing into the black veil of night. Without any hesitation she raced out of the window, cutting her hands and feet on the broken glass. She landed roughly on the frozen ground and felt her hands and feet burn as she ran. Screaming at the top of her lungs she ran as fast as she could into the darkness.

Into the dead of this freezing night she ran, trying to hear her son's voice but the air was still and silent. She ran until her body collapsed onto the cold pavement and refused to move. Every muscle burned and her lungs felt frozen. Under the light of a full moon and dim street lamp, she laid. Tears streaming down her face as she gasped for air. She cried,

"My baby... it took my baby."

Chapter One: A New Home...

Rays from the morning sun beamed through the frosted window of a messy room. Inside, nestled within the soft blankets of his bed, snored an eleven-year-old boy named Landon Brary.

The rising sun gently warmed his pale face and pulled him out of his slumber, waking him to the sounds of the new October day. Landon rolled off his pillow, stretched up, and reluctantly got out of his warm bed. He wiped the sleep from his eyes and straightened his red flannel pajamas before staggering over to his bedroom window. He peered down at the street below and yawned loudly. As he watched some of the younger children chase after one another on their way to school, he raised his hand and placed it on the glass. It was cold.

"Another new place with new people... bleh," sighed Landon as he rolled his eyes. "I hope this school is better than the last."

Over the course of a week, Landon and his family moved from their incredibly too small and too expensive apartment in New York city, into a beautiful red and white Queen Ann Victorian Grandeur in Colorado Springs. The beautiful home sat in the middle of a spacious cul-de-sac within the heart of a cozy little neighborhood called, Conroy Cove. Being the only child of his family, Landon usually got the small. However, this was not the case of his newest room. It was on the second floor, inside a turret peaking over the block, and it was the largest room in the entire house.

Landon's parents loved to travel, so they moved around a lot. Though he liked to see new places, he didn't care much for having to transfer to new schools and make new friends. Landon moved so often that he has lived in well over half of the states in the nation. However, this time was different. This was their first house and his parents bought it.

Being that it's his birthday, Landon loves Halloween. Yet, Christmas has always been his favorite holiday. So naturally,

Landon's favorite thing about his new home was the address, 25 December Drive.

Landon turned away from his window to see his bedroom door suddenly burst open. Happily barreling straight towards him was a howling white and brown Australian Sheppard.

"Jangers!"

Delighted by his dog's sudden entrance, Landon dropped to the floor as Jangers ran over to him. He wrapped his arms around the playful pup who responded joyfully by licking him all over his face. Jangers was so excited that not only did his nub of a tail wag, but so did his entire back end. Prompting Landon to refer to him as, 'Wiggle Butt'. Then, after a few rounds of wrestling, Landon picked himself up and sorted through some nearby laundry.

"What should I wear today Jangers?" Landon asked holding up one red and black striped shirt and one black shirt with a silver skull on it.

Jangers made a sound in between barking and howling, almost like he was talking to Landon. Then, turned and chased after his own tail.

"Yeah, that's what I thought too. Can't argue with stripes."

Landon threw on the striped shirt, a pair of black pants, and his tattered red skate shoes. As he tied his shoes, Jangers took the opportunity to knock him back onto the floor. After wrestling with Jangers a little more, he walked to his bathroom and started to comb his messy black hair.

Landon was a pale thin boy with sharp features. No matter how much time he spent in the sun, he never got any darker. He also never once got a sunburn. He splashed a little water on his face and stared into his eyes. Each one a different color. His left was crystal blue and his right, forest green. A condition known as Heterochromia iridium. He often stared in the mirror and wondered who he resembled the most between his parents. Truth be told, he didn't look much like either one of them.

Landon went back to his room and threw his backpack over his shoulders. Then he turned around, pointed sternly at Jangers, and said,

"Listen up, Wiggle Butt! We are in stealth mode. So, be quiet."

Quietly, Landon descended the stairs. Carefully placing each foot on the step below as to not make any sound. He was trying to keep his mother from hearing him and slip out the door before she made him take a jacket and whatever else she thought he needed with him on his first day at his new school.

Landon was four steps from the bottom of the stairs when he heard someone in the kitchen shake the box of dog treats. Landon's eyes widened. He looked over his should and up the stairs. Jangers was already racing carelessly down towards him. The happy pup plowed through Landon's legs and knocked him down face first onto the wooden floor below. Completely ruining his stealthy attempt to leave.

"Good morning, Landon. Get your butt in here and eat this breakfast I made for you. It's your favorite. A peanut butter and jelly waffle sandwich with bananas," commanded a sweet voice from within the kitchen.

Landon's mother, Moira Brary, was a slender woman with curly long brown hair, a smile so bright it could light up any room, and soft caramel skin always looked like she was glowing. Moira helped Landon up off of the floor and handed him a thick brown canvas jacket.

"It's freezing out today. Take this."

Landon reluctantly took the jacket and glared down at Jangers, who was now laying on his back with what looked like a slobbery smile on his face.

"Mom, it's like eighty-five degrees outside."

"Listen to your mother," said a deep voice from within the kitchen.

Staring over at Landon, a ruggedly handsome man in a sharp grey suit sat at a round glass table sipping coffee from a large orange pumpkin mug. His demeanor carried presence and certainty. Yet, the gleam in his soft eyes showed that he was kind and playful. Jensen Brary was Landon's hero.

"Good morning, son," said Jensen happily.

"Morning, Dad."

Landon took the coat that his mother had given him and tossed it over the back of his chair next to his dad. Jensen smiled as Landon took his seat, took a sip of his coffee, and sighed.

"Babe, did you read about the recent disappearance? It happened..."

"I know dear. I know," Moira interrupted, her wide eyes wide open as a signal for Jensen to stop speaking.

Landon sat quietly watching his parents speak without actually saying a word. They just stared at each other, nodding their heads in agreement. Then, after an awkward silence in which all three of them made eye contact, Jensen got up from his chair and walked over to Moira.

"Alright, I've got to get out of here. I'll call you when I pick Jared up from the airport after work."

"It's about time Uncle Jared got here," said Landon with a mouthful of waffle.

Jared Brary was Jensen's brother and Landon's only known living relative besides his parents. For as long as Landon could remember, Uncle Jared has always been around. As a matter of fact, the day Landon's parents brought him home he was there and has been with them ever since.

"That's what I'm saying," said Jensen as he kissed his wife and winked at Landon, grabbed the trash and made his way to the garage.

"Honey, don't forget about tonight," Moira shouted before Jensen shut the door.

"I'll be there. Love you, text me if you need anything."

Landon jumped out of his chair and raced out the door after his father. Jensen turned around and held out his hand placing it directly on the center of Landon's forehead as he tried to hug his father.

"Dad!" said Landon playfully as Jensen let his hand slip and wrapped his arms around Landon and squeezed tightly

"What? You thought I forgot about you? My favorite little man? Pssht! Love you, buddy. Have a great first day of school!"

"I will. Love you too, Dad," Landon replied.

"Now, if you'll excuse me. My baby is calling," Jensen said excitedly.

Jensen's baby was a black 1967 Chevy Impala that he often referred to as his batmobile. It became his dream car ever since he saw a T.V. show about two brothers who drove around the U.S. in a 1967 Chevy Impala investigating the supernatural. A show that quickly became a family favorite. Turns out that Uncle Jared even went to the same high school as one of the actors.

A few years back, while Jensen and Jared were on a road trip. They happened upon the Impala at a crossroads, Collins and Sheppard, in the middle of nowhere, abandoned. Jensen found a note on the windshield that said the car was free to whoever could start it and was signed Morgan Singer. The note still sits inside of the glove box and the Impala has been in the family ever since.

Landon waved goodbye and returned to the kitchen to finish what was left of his breakfast. Moira grabbed her cup of coffee, sat down at the table, and asked Landon curiously,

"Did you sleep well?"

"Not really. I had that dream again. I couldn't wake up... it always feels so real," Landon replied, shoving the last bit of waffle into his mouth.

"Well, it's over now. One day, you'll beat that nightmare."

"You think so?" Landon asked with his mouthful.

"I know so, honey. Anyway, you better get going too. You don't want to be late on your first day, my handsome young man," said Moira, leaning over and repeatedly giving Landon tiny kisses all over his shaggy head.

"Mom!"

"What? It's true. You are my handsome, young, little, tiny baby boy!" she laughed and took his plate.

Landon quickly got up before Moira could see him leave his jacket on the chair. He grabbed his backpack and darted to the front door.

"Bye, Mom!"

"What am I chopped liver? Get over here!" Moira shouted

She ran over and hugged him tightly before he could step out the door. Landon hugged her back, looked up and whispered,

"I love you too."

Landon stepped out onto the front porch and made his way through the leaf riddled yard. Standing on the sidewalk in front of Landon's house were a group of boys waiting for the school bus to come. Landon walked over to the bus stop and was instantly greeted by the not so friendly Roger Ivan Peters.

"Well, well, well. A new guy," sneered Roger.

Roger was the neighborhood bully. He was tall and lanky with straight brown hair that he wore in a short ponytail his head shaved underneath. He wore name brand clothing and was an only child that got anything he asked for from his parents. Roger should have been in high school but failed 8th grade and now had to repeat it.

Roger got his kicks by picking on kids smaller than him and playing cruel games. One of his favorite games to play called 'Grab and Go'. He would simply grab a kid's backpack and throw it into the street when a vehicle was coming.

"So, new guy. You wanna ride my bus?" Roger squeaked annoyingly.

Landon knew all too well the kind of kid he was. Over the years, Landon met all kinds of people and became quite the judge of character. Though it didn't take much for him to spot Roger's type. There was always a jerk or two at every new place he had been to. The kid that nobody liked but feared and tolerated.

Landon did not respond. He looked Roger dead in the eyes and pushed past him only to find himself standing in the middle of two grinning boys. It was obvious that they were Roger's goons.

They began circling around Landon like a pack of starving hyenas as Roger chuckled behind him.

A pale freckled boy with spiky blonde hair and braces named Nate Mitchell spit in front of Landon and asked,

"Hey little girl, gotta name?"

"Gotta toothbrush?" Landon responded and then covered his nose to avoid the stench of Nate's foul breath.

Nate clenched his jaw and balled his fists ready to swing. A thick boy, named Shirley Alec Kumar, reached out and stopped Nate before he could. He was tan with thin black greasy hair parted down the middle of his big round head. To Landon, Kumar's head looked like an oddly shaped mushroom growing out of his shoulders.

"Gotta pay the toll before you roll, sucka. Ten bucks!" Kumar demanded.

"Ten bucks?" Roger snorted.

"You'll need more than ten bucks to feed your fat ass,

Kumar! Twenty bucks, new guy. Or, I'm gonna have to stomp a

fool!"

Roger grabbed the strap of Landon's backpack and

wrenched it towards him. Immediately, Landon slipped out from

the strap and watched as Roger fell backward. Right onto his butt.

Nate and Kumar started to laugh. Then, Roger shot them an angry

look that silenced them both.

Standing closest to Roger was a young boy named Jake

Jackson. He had dark brown skin, piercing blue eyes, and long

tightly dreadlocked hair that hung down past his shoulders. He was

wearing black dusted jeans, red and white sneakers, a white polo,

and a black and white hooded letterman jacket. Jake had to practice

daily meditations. He convinced his parents to let him signed up

for Krav Maga classes with his brothers, but his parents insisted he

take weekly yoga classes and meditate for an hour once a day to

balance him. They also told him that if he gets into any fights that

aren't life or death Jake would be in serious trouble. Unfortunately,

Jake was also attached to the backpack that Roger used to pull himself up.

"What's wrong, brownie?" Roger asked obnoxiously as he smacked his hand down hard on Jake's shoulder.

"One, you're a racist. Two, you are an asshole. And three, move your hand or I will break three of your bones."

"Whoa! Check out this tough dread head! Don't mess with brother Buddha over here. He just started practicing krav magay." Roger shouted as he shoved Jake backward.

Landon went to grab his own backpack from the ground, but before he could get it, Roger's goons had already taken it. A yellow and black school bus turned onto the street and approached their stop.

"Bus is here!" Kumar yelled as he tossed the backpack to Roger.

"New guy, can't pay the toll? Then, pay the price!" Roger sneered as he threw Landon's backpack out onto the street.

They all watched as the backpack landed right in front of the school bus. Roger and his goons laughed loudly as a dark dirty tire rolled over it as the bus came to a stop.

"Sucks to be you!" Roger snickered.

Roger and his goons pushed past Jake and Landon and got onto the bus and. They continued their bullying by shoving the heads of random passengers as the irritating trio made their way to the back seats. Jake looked at Landon and shook his head, then reached down and grabbed Landon's backpack.

"What a douchebag," Jake said as he handed Landon the crushed backpack.

"I'm Jake by the way, Jake Jackson. Seventh grade. You?"

"Landon. Landon Brary. Yeah me too. Seventh grade I mean."

The two boys shook hands and then boarded the bus. They found a few empty seats towards the back far enough away that Roger and his goons held no interest in them. Once they arrived, Landon got off the bus and took in the view of his new school. It certainly didn't look like any school he had ever seen and it was definitely a lot nicer looking than his previous school. According to Jake, the school just opened its doors for students this year.

"Welcome to W.B. Watterson Middle School," Jake said as he exited the bus.

"What's the W. B. stand for?" Landon asked.

"I don't know. The school was named after some artist guy who had pet tiger or something like that. Anyway, I'll show you where the attendance office is so you can get a homeroom."

Landon followed Jake into the main office and waited to be assigned a homeroom. When it was his turn to speak to the attendance secretary, Jake convinced her to place Landon in his class. Jake had also taken the responsibility of showing him around the school for the week.

"Thanks, Jake," Landon said, happy to know somebody on his first day.

"No worries. Big Peach will give you your schedule with all the room numbers. It's not really hard to navigate the school.

Pretty simple. Anyway, this way." replied Jake motioning for Landon to follow him through the halls.

"Big Peach?" Landon questioned.

"Oh, that is what we call our teacher. Used to be Teach and then turned into Big Teach, until finally, Big Peach."

Landon, who was now even more confused about the Peach answer, followed Jake through the crowded halls and on more than one occasion had to dodge out of the way of kids tearing through the halls.

"It gets kinda crazy around here, " Jake shouted over the roaring hallway.

"I can see that," Landon whispered to himself.

The school may not have looked like any of the other schools Landon had attended, but the kids all seemed pretty much the same. Most of them leaned on the walls in small groups, throwing paper wads, hiding from bullies, or conversing with their friends while everyone else just seemed to roam the halls waiting for the final bell to ring.

Jake brought Landon to his homeroom class and the two of them made their way to a couple empty desks in the back. As they were settling into their seats, Landon noticed from the corner of his eye that somebody across the room was watching him. A pretty girl with curly auburn hair dressed in a black-and-white striped sweater dress was looking at Landon as he made his way to the seat.

The girl smiled then found her attention drawn to a quirky girl pulling on her arm and laughing at something she found in a letter.

"Who is that girl in the corner over there?" Landon asked.

"Oh, that's Alexia Sepulveda," Jake answered.

"You know her?"

"Yeah, we've been friends for a while now. Since third grade, I think. She's pretty cool. Not snobby or stuck up or anything. She's pretty chill." Jake answered.

Landon turned to find Jake rummaging through his backpack and pulling out all of its contents. Landon quickly grabbed the bag from Jake's hands and asked,

"What are you doing?"

"My bad. You got any food? I'm starving, man! Please, please, pretty please?" Jake asked, folding his hands into a steeple in front of his frowning face.

Landon sighed, then reached into his bag and found a squished cereal bar and handed it to Jake whose eyes instantly filled with delight.

"Thank you!" said Jake excitedly.

While Jake tore through the wrapper and stuffed the sweet honey cereal bar into his mouth, Landon returned his attention back to Alexia. She had smooth clear skin, big hazel eyes, and a captivating smile. Landon found his gaze tracing over her long flowing hair and pretty face, letting his eyes wander slowly until he found those big hazel eyes staring right back at him.

His heart jumped so fast it sounded like somebody set off a bomb inside of his chest. Short of breath and trying to conceal his dreamy stare, he tried his best to play it off as though he was deep in thought and then suddenly came to reach a solution to some dilemma he had been pondering.

He quickly pulled out his spiral notebook, a broken pencil, and tried to write something. Only nothing was coming to mind. So instead, he just scribbled and then admired it as though it was something that urgently needed to be transcribed, lest he forgets.

The sound of the last bell rang, sending kids eagerly running for their desks. A plump, balding man with a thick gray mustache grumbled as he waddled his way into the room full of restless children. He was wearing black slacks and a white long sleeve oxford shirt with suspenders that strained tightly over his belly. Held tightly in his pudgy hands, he carried a brown tattered briefcase and a notebook that read 'Lesson Planner'.

The man set his things upon a paper-strewn desk in the front of the classroom and then turned to the class. Placing his thumbs underneath the overly stretched suspenders, he silently stared at the class with a grumpy face. His beady little eyes narrowed as though he were trying to see through each and every one of the children in the classroom.

"Good morning class," he grumbled from behind his twitching mustache.

"We have a new student joining us today. So, allow me to make something perfectly clear!" he shouted to Landon directly.

"My name, young man, is Mr. Brevander! Not Mr. Beaver. Not Mr. Lavender. And, most certainly not, ever, Mr. B! Mr. Brevander is my name and I am your homeroom teacher. Apparently, I am also your history teacher." Mr. Brevander announced firmly.

Mr. Brevander then turned from Landon and paced through the rows of desks, making eye contact with each of his students as though they were all up to something suspicious.

"I will not tolerate any nonsense or Tom Foolery in my class. Anyone caught breaking school rules will serve detention with me after school. Which, I assure you, will make you think twice about ever coming back." said Mr. Brevander with an added tinge of sarcasm and a grin that made Landon completely uncomfortable.

Mr. Brevander picked up a stack of papers from his desk and raised them over his head and shook them in his little hands.

"Now, I have some items to issue out. When I call your name, raise your hand so I can see where you are."

While Mr. Brevander began to call out the names of the students Jake turned and nudged Landon.

"Hey, if Roger is in your gym class, stay far away from the restroom in the back. Keep to the front of the locker room where the coach is, otherwise… swirly city. Roger and his idiots will have you smellin' like the turd man!" Jake warned as he pulled up his hair and stared at Landon wide-eyed with a deeply concerned look upon his face.

Landon scrunched his face in disgust as Jake, eyes still wide and serious, leaned back in his chair and shook his head at the thought.

"I'm serious. Even worse, most don't get flushed until the end of the day. Gross!" Jake continued.

Landon's attention retreated after he heard a loud grumbling coming from his teacher.

"Brary... Landon Brary..."

Mr. Brevander was shaking a piece of paper violently above Landon's head. His plump face as red as a tomato as he angrily waited for Landon to answer him. Landon quickly snapped to the sound and shot his hand up into the air.

"Not too quick are you lad? Forget your name, did you? Well, it's written on this paper. So, memorize it! If you still cannot seem to remember it, then you can meet with me and write it on the dry-erase board one hundred times after school. What do you say?" snorted Mr. Brevander as he tossed the paper at Landon not waiting for him to answer.

Mr. Brevander turned back to the now snickering class and loudly cleared his throat, causing the room to become silent again.

"For those of you to whom I passed permission slips to, I need them signed and brought back by tomorrow. Otherwise, you will not be going to the wax museum next week to see the Halloween exhibit." Mr. Brevander commanded.

Twenty minutes later the bell rang and everyone piled out the door, seeking freedom from the grumpy cloud raining down on Mr. Brevander. Jake took Landon to his next class and agreed to meet up with him after.

"Room D203, Biology," Landon whispered to himself.

As he entered the classroom, his nose began to burn. A putrid stench stained the air, making it incredibly uncomfortable for Landon to breathe. As he searched for a place to sit, a squeaky voice came from across the room.

"Don't mind the smell. I am your Biology teacher. My name is Mrs. Freegwanalily. Free-gwan-ah-lily, okay?" squeaked a short, purple haired woman with a long sharp nose wearing a white lab coat and giant pink rubber gloves.

"Actually, you all should attempt to get used to it. The smell comes from formaldehyde and it is a unique liquid we used to keep our animal cadavers preserved," she explained while ushering the last of her students into the classroom.

"Good morning children. Welcome back and welcome to our new student, Landon. Now, listen for your names and raise your hand when I call you."

From the corner of his eye, Landon noticed someone quickly enter the classroom and race to the empty chair next to him. It was Alexia. She hurriedly placed her items under the chair and sat close to Landon, trying not to be seen. However, Mrs. Freegwanalily took notice right away and pointed a long, crooked finger at her. Squeaking loudly like a ferocious mouse she asked,

"Alexia! Why are you late to class?"

"I was here on time, but had to excuse myself because of the smell," Alexia replied softly as her face temporarily drained of blood.

Mrs. Freegwanalily turned her nose up into the air and sniffed loudly, as though the smell wasn't there. After a few seconds, she turned her eyes back to Alexia.

"As I stated before – get used to it. I trust this will be the first and last time you will be late to my class?" Mrs. Freegwanalily asked rhetorically.

"Today, we will begin our exploration of the pig anatomy. We will do so by dissecting a single cadaver that I have personally accounted for and assigned to each table."

Groaning could be heard as she turned away from the class to retrieve a small metal push cart with several silver trays. Each tray containing the body of a small piglet and a clear plastic box of surgical tools. Trying not to look too obvious, Landon subtly turned his eyes towards Alexia. Apparently, as subtle as he thought he was being when he made his way to look at her, she was staring right at him. Landon quickly opened his spiral notebook and started writing with his broken pencil. Alexia giggled quietly and then leaned in close and whispered,

"Hi, my name is Alexia."

"Hi, I'm…" but before Landon could say his name Alexia interrupted him.

"Landon, yeah I heard Mr. Brevander when he yelled your name, like, a million times."

As Landon and Alexia shared in a soft laughter, she pulled out a fully intact, unsharpened pencil from her backpack and handed it to Landon.

"What happened to your stuff?" Alexia asked.

"Some idiot threw my bag at the bus and it got run over," Landon huffed.

"Let me guess - Roger?" Alexia whispered as Landon's eyes spitefully narrowed.

"Yeah, that'd be the idiot."

Alexia shook her head and pretended to be writing notes as Mrs. Freegwanalily had taken notice of their conversation. Alexia's voice rang sweetly through his ears and Landon felt lost in the sound. Throughout the class, he zoned in and out of their conversation trying not to stare as they shared notes and listened to Mrs. Freegwanalily explain in great and unsettling detail how to dissect a pig.

Landon had never felt nervous talking to girls, but he found being near Alexia left his mind blank. During those moments, Alexia seemed to carry their conversation until his brain snapped back into working mode. Suddenly, the bell rang throughout the school and the children all scrambled towards the door.

"Next class we will begin to really dig into our cadavers. Be prepared to explore the beauty of anatomy!" Mrs. Freegwanalily yelled as her students raced out of the classroom.

"Fresh air! What class do you have now?" Alexia asked as they too quickly hurried to escape the stench of the classroom.

Landon reached into his front pocket and pulled out the class schedule that Mr. Brevander had given him.

"Um... let's see. Looks like gym," Landon answered.

"You want me to show you where it is? I have to go to Algebra and its right down the hall." Alexia asked with a smile.

"Yeah, that would be great," Landon said hoping to not sound too eager.

While they walked through the halls together, Landon couldn't help stealing a glance every now again until they eventually stopped outside a pair of gray metal doors.

"Here's the gym. Guess I'll see ya later?" Alexia asked.

"Cool," Landon replied with a smile.

And, with a smile still on her soft face, Alexia turned away from Landon and walked down the hall to her class. Landon sighed as he turned to the gym and pushed one of the doors open. Instantly, he felt himself shoved to the ground. An irritating voice echoed loudly through the gym, rattling Landon's nerves, and piercing his eardrums as he fell.

"Hey there, new guy!"

Landon looked up over his shoulder and saw Roger and his dimwitted lackeys laughing at him.

"New guy already got himself a girlfriend. Isn't that cute?" Roger said mockingly.

"Yeah, isn't that cu," Kumar repeated, but was interrupted by Roger's hand smacking him in the back of his head.

"I just said that, fat ass!"

"Ha! He went from new guy to ew guy," Nate shouted obnoxiously.

As Landon got up off the ground, Roger got right up in his face and whispered,

"Do something."

Landon dropped his bag and balled both of his fists. Just as he was about to swing, a thick strong hand pulled him effortlessly back from Roger and his goons.

"You!" commanded a deep booming voice that shocked the smirk right off of Roger's face.

"Go get suited up before I have y'all running laps for the rest of the week! And, you come with me. Now!"

Pulling Landon away from the scrambling goons was a tall and extremely muscular Samoan man wearing a blue athletic shirt that was clearly too tight and had 'Coach' boldly written across it. He pointed one massive finger and said sternly,

"Office."

Landon quickly made his way into the Coach's office and was immediately seated on a stool in front of an old beat-up metal desk. Coach walked behind the desk and threw his massive body down onto a burgundy chair and stared at Landon. He stared silently for a few moments and then with one eyebrow cocked up high he asked,

"What's your name, kid?"

"Landon Brary, sir," he replied.

The enormous man leaned back in his chair and crossed his massive arms, turning away from Landon and looking into the gym through the dirty window by his desk.

"Sir? I like that. The name's Douglas Anderson. Just call me Coach, understood?"

"Yes, Coach."

Coach turned back around and raised two massive fingers up in front of Landon like a peace sign.

"Two rules. The first, no fighting," Coach stated as he pulled his middle finger down. "The second, don't break rule number one, understood?"

"Yes, Coach," Landon repeated.

"You wear a medium shirt and shorts?" Coach asked as he reached into a locker behind him, grabbed uniform.

"Yes, I think so."

"Be out in five," Coach ordered, nodding towards the locker room.

Landon headed for the locker room and instantly remembered Jake's advice to stay in the front, away from Roger and his goons.

Throughout the class, Landon stayed as far from Roger as possible. He did pretty well until they ended up having to be on the same team while playing dodgeball. Roger didn't hesitate to take advantage of any opportunity to harass Landon. He did so by pushing him into other teammates, stepping on his feet, and shoving him into nearby walls when Coach was distracted.

However, Landon also took advantage of Coach being distracted and used these opportunities to throw the dodgeball as hard as he could at the back of Roger's head.

The other children looked on in amazement as Landon repeatedly smashed Roger with furiously thrown red balls. There was even a moment when Roger turned around and a wild dodgeball hit him right in the face. Landon thought he saw Roger's eyes tear up, but he turned and ran away into the locker room. Then, Coach blew his whistle, stopped everyone in their tracks, and shouted,

"Great effort out there today. Hit the showers, get ready for your next class, and, make sure you take your uniforms home. Not just home either, Jason. Make sure you wash them! Coach don't run no stank nasty gym,"

As Landon headed towards the locker room, a few of his classmates ran up and began to express their delight in watching him stand up to Roger. Each one reveling in watching Landon give Roger a taste of his own medicine. Landon quietly listened as they walked alongside him and reenacted a dodgeball smashing into Roger's head in slow motion. Just as they all entered the locker room, Roger grabbed Landon by his shirt and slammed him against the lockers.

"Think you're pretty funny eh, new guy?" Roger snorted.

Landon tried to push Roger off but was instantly slammed back against the lockers by both Nate and Kumar.

"Hey, what's that smell?" Roger asked his goons sarcastically.

Then, right on Roger's cue, Kumar leaned in and sniffed loudly next to Landon,

"Ugh, I think it's the new guy!"

"Smells like shit." Nate answered as he too sniffed at Landon.

"New guy needs a bath. We can help him, right?" Roger said as he nodded to the restroom.

Nate and Kumar eagerly pulled Landon off of the lockers and pushed him into the restroom, moving him towards the closest stall. Landon kicked and twisted his body trying with all his might to get himself free. Roger kicked the door open and started to laugh.

"Hey, would ya look at that?"

A foul wave of urine filled Landon's nostrils and made him choke a little. As he tried to look away Roger grabbed his head and pushed it down close to the toilet. Inside, floating in dark yellow water he saw something big and brown.

"Listen, we are only trying to help. You don't want to look shitty for your girl, right?" Roger whispered.

"Let go of me!" Landon yelled, kicking Nate in the chest as hard as he could.

Landon felt Nate's hand slip and pulled his leg free and kicked Kumar's groin, knocking him over and leaving him gasping for air on the tile floor. Roger tried to keep ahold of Landon but it was too late. He had both legs free and dropped them to the ground. Landon quickly tucked himself down to the ground and rolled backwards away from the stall. He then sprung back up to his feet and came face to face with Roger.

Roger swung a wild fist and socked Landon in his right eye. Pain shocked his whole body and filled him with rage. Roger quickly reached out to grab Landon's head and force it into the toilet bowl but he dodged his attempt and punched Roger as hard as he could, right in the stomach. He hit him so hard he knocked all the air out his lungs.

As Roger clamored for air he tripped on his own feet and went tumbling backward, right into the unflushed toilet. Suddenly, a loud cheer erupted from behind Landon. All of the kids had gathered to watch the fight and were now clapping and laughing as Roger sat stuck in the toilet, struggling to breathe and lift himself out.

Instantly, the cheering was silenced. Coach pushed his way through the crowd of cheering kids and walked into the restroom. He saw Nate and Kumar pulling themselves up from the ground and Roger desperately trying to lift himself out of the toilet. He then turned to Landon, noticing his eye was a bright shade of red and swollen, and asked,

"What was rule number one?"

"No fighting," Landon answered regretfully.

Landon moved out of the way as Coach reached down and pulled Roger out of the toilet and onto his feet.

"So, what happened?" Coach asked, but no one responded.

"If someone doesn't start talking, laps will be the last thing you have to worry about," Coach said, crossing his muscular arms as he waited for an answer.

Coach stared at Landon and raised one eyebrow as a kind of cue for him to start talking. Landon looked down at Roger. He was shaking his head and gritting his teeth. He could read from Roger's face that he did not want him to tell Coach what had actually happened. Landon looked back up at Coach and began to tell him the only thing he could think of to keep him out of trouble - a lie.

"Coach, it wasn't a fight. Truth is, I noticed that Roger was trying to show Nate and Kumar some kind of dance moves but they ended up running into each other which made Roger fall into the toilet. I saw it and just came in here to help."

"You expect me to believe that?" Coach asked as he lowered his eyebrows and leaned down about an inch away from Landon's face.

"What happened to your eye then?" Coach questioned.

Landon reached up, touched his swelling eye, and pretended not to be surprised as he flinched with pain.

"Oh, that must have happened when we were playing dodgeball."

"What about you Roger? Is that what happened? Because, if I find out you were all fighting, we would have a big problem." Coach asked suspiciously.

"It's true. I was trying to teach them how to do a dance move."

Coach then leaned over to Roger, quickly turning his nose away with a scrunched-up face and said sternly,

"You had better go and change back into your gym clothes. Unless you want to smell like that all day?"

Coach motioned for the crowd to disperse and waited until the three bullies made their way back into the locker room. Before Landon could walk past him, Coach turned and placed one of his large calloused hands on Landon's shoulder.

"If there's one thing I'm not, it's an idiot," Coach said with a smile as he gently pushed Landon back into the locker room.

"Hurry up or you'll be late to your next class."

Coach went back to his office, sat down in his worn-out chair, and began to toss a football up into the air. As the Roger, Kumar, and Nate made their way past Landon and the office, Coach snapped his thick fingers and yelled out,

"This is gym, not a dance!"

When Roger was sure he was far enough away from Coach's office that he could not hear him, he turned to Landon with balled his fists and whispered,

"You're a dead man, new guy."

Landon slowly leaned in towards Roger, sniffed loudly, and with a scrunched face he replied in disgust,

"You're so full of shit, Roger. And, you smell like it too."

Word had traveled fast of the events that transpired during gym class and even more so about the toilet incident within the locker room. Landon spent the rest of his day meeting new people who were eager to hear about what had happened in the locker room. He had won a kind of instant popularity for standing up to Roger and his goons.

School ended and as he started to head for the buses he found Jake waiting for him on the sidewalk. He had heard about what had happened with Landon but he did not seem as thrilled as all the other kids were. In fact, he advised Landon of how Roger will most likely try to kill him now so he should walk home and then fake sick for a month in hopes that Roger might forget about him and move onto some new victim. Landon was listening, but truthfully, Roger was the last thing on his mind. All he could think about was Alexia and how he couldn't wait to see if she had any other classes with him. By the end of Jake's rant, he convinced Landon that they should walk home instead of taking the bus where he was sure Roger would be waiting.

They finally made it to their street and as it turned out Jake was his neighbor, living in the house just to the right of his. The two said goodbye, but not before Jake once again tried with all his being to convince Landon to not ride the bus in the morning.

Landon went inside, set his things down, and went to the kitchen where he made a himself a waffle sandwich and retrieved a list of daily chores from the refrigerator. After finishing the chores, he played with Jangers, watched some movies, and waited for his parents to come home from work.

Landon laid down and stretched himself out on the couch, feeling his body sink into the soft pillows. He smiled and looked up at a large wooden grandfather clock that stood tall in the corner of the living room. Landon watched as the pendulum swung smoothly back and forth, all the while thinking about Alexia. As he closed his eyes to fall asleep, Landon whispered to Jangers,

"Tomorrow can't come any faster, Jangito."

Chapter Three: Day Dreamer…

Black smoke rolled over the neon green grass and began choking the air all around Landon. He coughed and gasped, straining desperately to breathe. Something was moving from within the swelling smoke slowly engulfing the world around him. As his heart raced, the screams of crying infants started to ring through the darkness like an eerie choir of broken church bells.

"I won't let you have him!" shouted a muffled voice from within the smoke.

The voice faded and was quickly replaced by a wicked laughter that pierced Landon's ears. The smoke violently wrapped around his body and pulled him onto the freezing ground. He tried with all his might to move but could feel his body being effortlessly restrained by the smoke.

Suddenly, less than an inch from Landon's face, were two blazing emerald eyes burning wildly from within the thick black smoke. Below the fiery eyes was a salivating mouthful of long, razor sharp, silver teeth grinning through the darkness. The grinning teeth opened widely and started to suck in the air. It made a haunting sound and began pulling something from under Landon's skin, something deep beneath the tissue of his muscles and the marrow of his bones. It felt like it was pulling out the very essence of his being.

Landon's body writhed in waves of pain and darkness quickly consumed his vision. His body became limp and his lungs and throat burned from choking on the thick smoke. He felt helpless and weak. It felt like he was about to die.

A burst of white light seared through the darkness and beamed brightly upon his blurred vision. Landon shot up off of the couch, throwing the pillow violently off of him as he made his way over the magical crossing of dreams back to reality. Shivering in cold sweat and breathing heavily, a soothing voice cut through the chaos and calmed his nerves.

"It's okay, sweetheart. I'm right here. It was just a dream. Shh, everything is fine." Moira said softly as she laid him gently back on the couch.

"Mom?"

"Yes honey. Same nightmare?" Moira asked.

Landon pulled himself together, took a sip from a glass of water his mother handed to him and whispered,

"It always feels… so real,"

"My brave boy, you have such a powerful imagination. I should have woken you up a long time ago."

"It's okay Mom. I slept well. Just a stupid nightmare. I'm fine," Landon said sleepily.

"Well, then I'm going to go and start making breakfast. Any special requests?"

"Maybe your famous avocado toast and potatoes?" Landon answered.

"Excellent choice! That is exactly what I wanted this morning too."

Landon pulled himself off of the couch and walked up to his bedroom where he found Jangers waiting outside the door with his long tongue hanging out of the side of his mouth, smiling.

Apparently, the pup had been waiting at the door for some time because a puddle of drool found its way under the door and Landon's foot.

"So gross," Landon said while shaking his foot.

As he opened the door, Jangers ran right into the room and immediately began chewing on one of Landon's slippers.

"Good morning to you too, Puppers. You probably have great dreams, huh? Catching cats and chewing on all kinds of stuff. Lucky dog."

After wiping his foot clean with a dirty shirt, Landon walked over to the window and looked outside. Once again, he placed his hand upon the glass to feel how cold he thought it was and then went to shower. After he finished getting dressed, he walked downstairs to the kitchen where his mother had breakfast waiting.

Jensen came into the kitchen and sat down at the table with his usual a cup of coffee. He loved his coffee, especially because of all his unique mugs and cups. Today's mug was a combination of Halloween monster faces.

"Good morning, buddy. Ready for your second day of school?" Jensen asked.

"Yeah, it's pretty cool so far." Landon said with half a taco shoved into his mouth.

"That's my boy. Listen, your mother and I will be home late today, so text us when you get home. I want you to lock all the doors and windows and be sure to set the alarm. Uncle Jared may come by, he is the only person you let in, okay?"

Landon nodded and shoved the rest of the taco into his mouth. The doorbell rang and Moira went to the window. She pulled open the curtain and saw Jake standing outside the front door, wrapped up in a green puffer jacket and a red scarf.

"Landon, I believe you have a friend waiting for you outside," Moira said as she handed him his lunch along with his coat.

"Thanks, Mom," Landon huffed.

"Bye, Dad. I Love you both."

As soon as Moira turned her back Landon threw his coat on the coat rack and darted out the door. Instantly, Landon saw a worried expression on Jake's face which he kept as they began walking towards the bus stop.

"Seriously? You're going to ride the bus?" Jake asked.

"Yep."

Roger and his goons were eagerly waiting as they approached the bus stop. Roger pointed at Landon, traced his finger from one side of his neck to the other, and shouted,

"Dead man walking."

Landon stopped, lifted his shoes one at a time and inspected the bottoms of them. Then he looked over at Jake and asked loudly,

"Do you smell that?"

Jake quickly checked his shoes too but found them clean. He tried sniffing the air but smelled nothing. Jake looked back at Landon awkwardly and shrugged his shoulders, not knowing what he supposed to smell. Before he could ask, Landon looked over and pointed at Roger,

"Smells like shit."

Jake's eyes widened and Landon laughed. Suddenly, Roger and his goons darted towards them. Nate and Kumar went after and Roger tackled Landon to the ground. As Roger crashed into him, Landon slammed his forehead into Roger's nose. They hit the ground and Landon pushed Roger off of him. Kumar turned his attention away from Jake and kicked Landon in the back sending a shockwave of pain down his spine.

Jake was too fast for Roger's goons and easily dodged their wild swinging fists. When Kumar turned around to help Roger, Jake side kicked Nate in the stomach and dropped the freckled bully to his knees. Jake turned to Kumar and landed a stunning punch under Kumar's chin that made him instantly dizzy. Landon pushed Kumar's leg back and watched him fall over. He quickly got to his feet and saw Roger balling his fists. Landon swung a wild fist Roger and felt something crunch under his knuckles.

Suddenly, Roger's eyes watered and his nose started to pour blood. Kumar regained his footing and punched Landon in his chest. Jake caught Landon as he stumbled backwards and stopped him from falling down. Kumar tried to Kick Landon but he caught it as Jake kicked his other leg out from under him. Kumar screamed as he dropped into the splits, ripped his pants, and farted.

Both of them let out a hearty laughter only for it to be quickly interrupted by Roger punching Landon in his jaw. Landon dropped to a knee picked himself up, only to be knocked back down to one knee from Roger punching him again.

"Get up!" Roger screamed sharply.

As Landon pulled himself up he reached into his backpack and pulled out his Biology textbook. Just as Roger swung at him again, Landon met his fist with the cover of his textbook. Instantly there was a loud snap. Roger immediately dropped to his knees and howled,

"You broke it! You broke my hand!"

Kumar and Nate stopped fighting and ran over to Roger who was both crying and bleeding all over himself. Jake grabbed Landon by his collar, pulled him away from Roger, and together they ran.

Landon and Jake didn't stop running until they were halfway to school and were certain none of the bullies were following them. Out of breath and their legs feeling like they were on fire, they finally slowed down and started to walk. In between gasps of breath, they both began to laugh.

"That was… AWESOME!" Jake shouted.

Landon both smiled and cringed in pain between breaths and laughter as they walked. Since meeting Roger, he now not only had a bruised eye but also a swollen lip and a jaw that hurt when he talked.

"My mom is going to kill me. She already doesn't want me to play dodgeball anymore because she thinks I got my eye hurt from playing yesterday. How am I going to explain a bruised jaw?" Landon asked rhetorically.

"Yeah, maybe. But, you know what?" Jake asked.

"What?"

"If Roger's hand is really broken, it's not likely he will be picking on anybody anytime soon. Come on, we gotta hurry up and get to school, otherwise my parents are gonna kill me too!" Jake laughed, pulling Landon into a jog.

The boys eventually made it to school, purposefully taken the long way to their homeroom class in order to avoid seeing Roger's goons. On the way, Landon suddenly remembered the Alexia was in their class. He quickened their pace and actually walked into the classroom right as the bell rang. They hurried to their seats Landon noticed Alexia was not in the room.

After enduring Mr. Brevander's grumpy wrath and lecture on timeliness for what seemed like the entirety of the class, the bell finally rang. As they left, Landon pulled out his schedule and saw his next class was his least favorite subject - math. Before splitting off in different directions Landon and Jake confirmed they had lunch together and agreed to meet at the cafeteria. Landon looked back down at his schedule and sighed,

"Algebra… ugh. As if my head doesn't hurt enough already."

Landon eventually found the door to his next classroom, quietly stepped inside, and discovered the entire class staring at him.

"May I help you?" asked a younger looking man with thick brown hair and a bright smile.

"Um… is this algebra, sir?" Landon asked nervously.

"Well, you can cut that 'sir' stuff out in here. My name is Brian Cooley, a. k. a. Maverick, a. k. a. Mr. Cools. The latter is the preferred around my fellow employees. Welcome to my classroom! What's your name?"

"My name is Landon Brary," Landon answered.

Mr. Cools extended his hand for Landon to shake and then showed him to a desk before walking back to the front of the class and wiping the dry erase board clean.

"Okay everyone, close your books. In the spirit of having our new student, Landon, join our class. We are going to take the day off and get to know him."

The class cheered and quickly did as Mr. Cools instructed. It made Landon feel welcomed and eased his nerves, making him doubt his previous disdain for this math class.

"They don't call me Mr. Cools for nothing," Mr. Cools said with a wink.

For the rest of the class everyone enjoyed playing games and getting to know Landon. By the time the bell rang, he had made a few new friends and completely forgotten about his fight with Roger.

While wandering through the halls, Landon checked his schedule for his next class.

"Woodshop 101, room D210," Landon mumbled as he searched the numbers on each door he passed.

"What was that?" said a soft voice from behind him.

Landon turned to see Alexia smiling at him and completely derailing his train of thought.

"I… um… I have Woodshop," Landon stammered.

He could see she was staring at his swollen lip but she did not ask about it. Instead, she walked on the opposite side of it and looked over his schedule with him.

"I have Theater Arts right now. You want to walk with me?" Alexia asked.

Landon smiled and slightly nodded. Jake caught up with them on the way and began telling Alexia about what happened at the bus stop and Roger's hand. Landon could tell she wasn't impressed but was somewhat interested. They reached Alexia's class and before she entered, she asked,

"Jake and I have 2nd lunch, do you?"

"Actually, I do," Landon replied happily.

Alexia smiled at Landon and then closed the door.

"Where are you headed, Jake?"

"The most boring class ever made... Woodshop. Man, that class is the worst. Mr. Hawke has, like, no variation in his tone when he speaks. Like, none. It'll straight put you to sleep." Jake replied with a long sigh

"Check it out. We can be bored together," Landon said as he pointed to his schedule.

"Hey! We're bored buddies. Get it? Board buddies?"

"Nice dad joke." Landon laughed.

As they made their way to their next class, Jake lowered his voice to a whisper that was about as loud as his normal voice, only breathy.

"You think you will get in trouble for breaking Roger's hand?"

Landon had not even considered what his parents would do once they found out, if they found out. His mood shifted, and he pictured the trouble he would be in. He would probably have to go and apologize and then he would surely be punished. Punishments in the Brary house were creative and always had to do with some kind of physical labor or chore followed by a family discussion and ending with him usually losing a privilege or two for a few days.

"I don't even want to think about it. Besides, he got what he deserved,"

Landon answered.

The boys entered their next class and took a seat at a table in the back of the room. A thick and solid man wearing tan canvas overalls and a long sleeve red flannel button up shirt. He closed the door with his fuzzy hand and then sat down quietly at his desk in the front of the classroom. The bell rang and from behind his desk he started with the day's lesson for the class.

Jake's description of the class and Mr. Hawke was an understatement. Mr. Hawke droned on about the proper construction of their next project and how making a birdhouse would better the environment in a completely monotone voice that could put anyone to sleep. And in fact, it did. Landon felt the powerful effects of this monotone sleep spell and could do nothing to stop his eyelids becoming too heavy to keep open. The sounds in the room began to muffle and a quiet melody started to fill Landon's head as the world around him faded.

A soft lullaby chimed sweetly, soothing his nerves. Landon opened his eyes to a beautiful woman smiling down at him and humming to the tune. He took a look around and he was in a room laying in a wooden crib. The woman gently tucked him into some blankets, kissed him on his forehead, and then turned out the lights as she left the room.

"I love you so much," she whispered.

A galaxy of moons, planets, and stars danced above Landon while the chimes of the sweet lullaby continued to play softly through the darkness. He stared at the twinkling lights as they changed colors and watched an astronaut fly across his room on a rocket. His eyes traced over the ceiling and down the walls, until something from the corner of the room caught his eye.

In a corner across the room, sat an oval mirror wrapped in an iron frame. Landon could barely see the mirror's reflection, but it looked like it was rippling. Suddenly, a voice came from in front

of the crib and an extremely tall, goofy looking man, with long and

wild red hair, leaned over Landon and smiled from ear to ear,

literally.

    "Hi," he said warmly.

    "I'm Simon, Simon Hush. It is truly my honor nice to meet

you, Landon."

    As startling as Simon was, Landon did not feel afraid. He

looked into Simon's big purple eyes and saw kindness. Simon's

long hair fell onto Landon's face and tickled his nose, causing him

to giggle. Simon laughed, pulled his hair back from Landon's face,

and tried to tie it back with more of his hair.

    "It has got a mind of its own."

    Suddenly, the temperature in the room dropped. Landon

looked over Simon's shoulder and saw two small green lights

flickering in the mirror's rippling reflection. Ice started to crawl

like frozen veins from out of the mirror, across the walls and

ceiling of the room. Simon was now aware of the temperature drop and had taken notice of the ice now spreading across the room. As he traced the ice back to the mirror, he saw a dark smoke pouring out of it. As it filled the room, the smoke quickly swallowed the tiny lights above them.

Out of the swelling darkness, a pale skeletal face with blazing eyes of emerald fire appeared in front of Simon. Thin strands of saliva dripped down it's long, razor sharp, silver teeth and onto Simon's face.

"What are you?"

Simon's voice was instantly muffled by a rotten hand wrapping tightly around his face and was replaced by a wicked laughter that sent chills down Landon's spine. It pushed Simon to his knees and leaned over the crib. He could see the ice starting to creep onto his bedding. Landon tried to scream but his lungs were immediately flooded with smoke and choked his cries. Like a rogue wave, panic rose and overwhelmed every nerve in Landon's body as it leaned directly over Landon, opened its terrifying mouth full of razor sharp teeth, and started to suck in the air around him. The sound scratched at his eardrums like nails dragging slowly across a chalk board.

A sparkling indigo mist rose from his body and was sucked into the eyes, nasal cavity, and mouth of the skeletal face. Landon felt his very essence being drained. It felt like he was burning from the inside out. Simon picked himself up from the floor and reached out his long hands and wrapped his fingers around the skeletal face. Simon dug his fingers into its hollow eye sockets and with all his might, wrenched it away from Landon.

"Get away from him!" Simon screamed.

The smoke left Landon's lungs and started to wrap around Simon. As it did, the room shook and the windows cracked. The smoke was spinning like a tornado and there were flashes of purple and green lights exploding across the smoke like a lightning storm. Landon could no longer see Simon, but he could hear him screaming.

Suddenly, a bright white light cut across the ceiling and ripped through the darkness, illuminating the entire room. The *smoke quickly retreated into the mirror and pulled Simon with it,*

leaving the surface rippling like a stone cast into a calm lake.

Landon felt the warmth of a woman's hands quickly pick

him up from the floor and cradle him to her chest. It was the same

woman who tucked him in. She rocked back and forth, tears

welling up in her eyes, her face stricken with concern as she called

out to a man who quickly ran into the room.

"Where is he?" asked the man.

"I've got him. I can't do this again. What if..." she tried to

say, but the man interrupted her before she could finish.

"It won't."

"We are running out of time," she said sternly.

Suddenly, the loud snap of a long thick wooden ruler jolted

Landon from his slumber. He quickly sat upright, rubbing the sleep

from his eyes. His heart pounded and a light mist of a cold sweat

glistened across his forehead and cheeks. The shock of waking up

so abruptly made it incredibly difficult for Landon to recognize

where he was and even worse, calm himself down. His breathing was shallow and his throat dry. His eyes stung and he felt dizzy.

Landon shot up from his seat, coughing and then taking in some lung filling breaths. It only took a few moments, but after his eyes cleared, his mind quickly followed.

"Are you okay," Mr. Hawke asked somewhat insensitively.

"I will be."

"Well then, Mister... Mister... um... who are you and why are you sleeping in my class?"

"He's new. His name is Landon Brary," Jake quickly responded.

"Well then. Mr. Berry, am I boring you?"

"No, sir," Landon replied.

Mr. Hawke stared at Landon for an uncomfortable amount of time before turning back to the front of the room and then lecturing the class on the importance of being able to work with your hands. Landon looked over at Jake, who was staring right at him, and whispered sarcastically,

"Thanks for waking me up, Board Buddy!"

"You can't just pass out in class, man. Mr. Hawke's boring, but he sees everything," Jake whispered back, lowering his head to hide from Mr. Hawke as he looked over.

"That would've been good to know, Jake."

Mr. Hawke separated the class into groups and handed each one instructions on how to build a toolbox. Landon and Jake tried to read the instructions, but Mr. Hawke's handwriting was comparable to that of a child just learning to write. Before Mr. Hawke could begin a new lecture, a voice with a subtle Spanish accent echoed throughout the school over the loudspeaker.

"Good afternoon ladies and gentlemen. This is Principal Gonzalez speaking. In fifteen minutes, we will have a school assembly. All staff and students will meet in the school auditorium. That is all. Thank you."

The class was released and everyone made their way to the auditorium. Landon and Jake spotted Alexia, who had saved seats for them, and sat down next to her. Teachers made several attempts to quiet the roaring students, but eventually gave up and grouped together to converse with one another instead.

Landon could see Kumar and Nate picking on a couple of the younger kids until they caught Coach staring at them with his muscular arms crossed over his huge chest, slowly raising one eyebrow. He lifted two large fingers from his giant fist and pointed at his eyes and then at Kumar and Nate, making sure they knew he was watching. Both boys quickly ran over to their seats and sat down quietly. Landon chuckled as he watched them sink deep into their seats, hiding from Coach's stare.

The crowd roared on and Coach took the stage. He marched right to the center and loudly blew his silver whistle. The crowd, including the staff, immediately became silent. Coach smiled and said in a calm tone,

"They're all yours, Ollie."

Landon watched as Principal Gonzalez walked confidently to the center of the stage. As she walked by, he caught Jake staring at her with his mouth wide open. Tears were welling up in his eyes because he refused to blink. Jake quickly took notice of Alexia and Landon staring at him and snapped his mouth closed. As he repeatedly blinked to refresh his eyes, Jake smiled a toothy grin and nodded his head at Landon.

"Good afternoon students. I have called you all down here to advise you of a new safety policy that we are implementing here at our wonderful school. Over the past few weeks there has been a growing number of missing children in our city. I have spoken with many of your parents and we have all agreed that to protect you all, certain safety precautions must be introduced."

Her face stricken with concern, Mrs. Gonzalez paced slowly back and forth across the stage. She came to a stop, silently looked over the crowd of students, and then held up one finger.

"From now on, each student will be assigned a person from each class to be your buddy. This is called 'The Buddy Initiative' and it will be part of our daily procedures here a W.B. Watterson. Your buddy is responsible for escorting you to the cafeteria before departing for your next class where you will meet with your next buddy. And, so on and so forth."

Waves of whispers began to roll over the auditorium as the students started seeking friends to be their buddies. As the sound grew into a soft rumble, Coach stepped forward onto the stage, lifted one eyebrow, and cleared his throat. Once again rendering the auditorium silent.

"Thank you, Coach. Now, your homeroom teachers have been over here working to assign buddies from the list that my faculty and I have created. Let me be perfectly clear - there will be no trading of buddies." Mrs. Gonzalez said, causing the students to sigh in their disappointment.

"Here is the most important part of this speech. Each of you should pick a friend or, better yet, a group of friends to walk home with or ride the bus with when school lets out to ensure each of you get home safely. From now on, teachers will wait outside with our police liaison at the bus stop area and the student drop off area in front of the school. They will be there two hours before classes begin and two hours after they end."

Mrs. Gonzalez stopped pacing and for a moment she silently stared out at the students, lost in a thought. No one said a word. Everyone could clearly sense that a moment of sincerity rested upon her lips and in a much softer tone than she had just been using, Mrs. Gonzalez broke the silence.

"Please, believe me when I say this. Children, the world can be great and there is a lot out there for each one of you to enjoy, but there are some that want only to cause pain and suffering. Three students within our neighboring schools have gone missing, along with several more in our city. Now, I may only be your Principal, but I honestly care about your wellbeing and your futures," Mrs. Gonzalez said softly.

The tears she tried to hold victoriously won their freedom and fell like tiny raindrops onto her cheeks. Coach gently placed his giant hand on her shoulder. Mrs. Gonzalez turned from the crowd and into Coach's massive arms, sobbing softly into his chest.

"You are all released to your homeroom teachers. Thank you," Coach said as he escorted Mrs. Gonzalez off of the stage.

Alexia and Jake turned to Landon and at the same time, they both spoke the same words.

"Her son, David, was one of the kids that disappeared."

Before Landon could respond, Mr. Brevander began impatiently ushering the class back to their room. Once they were all seated at their desks, he started handing out each students' buddy list. Landon, Alexia, and Jake all received their lists. Immediately they began comparing and reading over them.

"Jake Jackson for homeroom, Catherine Klein for Algebra, Carlos Herrera for English, Dustin Spooner for Biology, Sith Saeng-on for Lunch, Doris Walters for History, Khary Alexander for music, Tommy Zanellato for Woodshop, Jeremy Patterson for Theater Arts, Sam Lotfi for Arts and..." Landon's face instantly formed into a scowl as he read the last name aloud,

"Roger Peters for Gym."

Jake and Alexia folded their lists and remained quiet. Neither of them knew what to say. The bell rang and Jake walked with Landon to the bus, trying to come up with a plan to get

Landon's list changed or somehow convince Coach to change his class to a different period.

"Well, at least you got a pretty good list. Dustin is hilarious, Jeremy is super chill, and Doris is an absolute sweetheart! Seriously, man, she is the nicest person I have ever known," Jake said trying his best to cheer up Landon.

"Yeah, I have known her and Chris forever. They are both really nice." Alexia added.

"Hey, you ride our bus too?" Landon asked, attempting to stifle his excitement.

"Yeah, I live down the street from Jake."

"It's over here you guys," Jake shouted as he ran ahead to the bus.

Landon, Jake, and Alexia entered the bus and as they made their way to the back Landon thought about Mrs. Gonzalez and her missing son.

"So, what happened to Mrs. Gonzalez's son?" Landon asked.

"Well, nobody really knows. When the first kid went missing, everyone thought that maybe she ran away. Next two sisters disappeared. Then, another and another. I heard the police weren't doing much to find out what was happening. But, this last time when David went missing the police finally started to suspect all the missing kids were being kidnapped," Alexia said.

"I knew those sisters that disappeared. Susie and Megan. We used to go to Elementary School with together. They always did everything together. They were inseparable, like best friends. They were even super tight with their parents, Glenda and Duane. Just a super cool family, ya know? They were always nice and brought the best vegan food! Anyway, about two weeks ago, they left school together and never made it home. I also know another kid that has disappeared. His name is Daniel Logan, lives in the neighborhood next to ours. Few weeks ago, he was taking out the trash and never came back inside. When his parents came looking for him, all they found was his Dallas Cowboys hat and a small pool of blood," Jake explained.

"Nobody knows if that's true," Alexia interrupted.

"Well, Jason said he was walking with Oscar to the old Conroy park and saw the blood stain on the concrete. I know them both pretty well and I don't think they would lie to me," Jake snapped.

Landon noticed a few of the other kids had started to eavesdrop on their conversation and listened intently as Jake continued his story.

"Rumor has it that the police believed that these missing kids were part of some runaway gang or some kind of stunt. That was until Mrs. G's kid went missing."

"Why wouldn't anyone think he ran away?" Landon asked.

"You don't know this because you just got here but, Mrs. G's was the chief of police, but he passed away last month. David's parents pretty much knew everyone around here. His parents, especially his dad, loved him and he was honestly happy. His dad was the coolest. David had no reason to run away," Jake replied.

"After David disappeared, the police launched their investigation. They think it is someone or a group of people kidnapping kids," Alexia added.

"Yep. That just kicked off a few weeks back. So, there's the believable kidnapping thing and then, of course, there are also a few other crazy rumors going around."

"Like what?" Landon asked.

"Well, there's one about some of the school janitors, an evil circus, oh and even alien abductions. But, the lamest rumor is about something that hides in the shadows and comes out at night. Like some kind of monster or something," Jake said with a light chuckle.

"A monster?"

"Yeah, it's so dumb. Here's our stop. Let's go, bus buddy!" Jake said before pulling on Landon's shoulder to get up as the bus approached their stop.

"So, Alexia… see you tomorrow?"

"Yeah, see you tomorrow," Alexia answered sweetly to Landon.

The boys waved goodbye and exited the bus. Then, after agreeing to meet up the next morning they went their separate ways. As Landon opened his door, he heard Jake yell out from his yard,

"Hey! Don't take the trash out alone or the monster will get ya!"

Landon smiled and gave Jake a cheesy smile with two thumbs up and then shut the door as he entered his home. He locked the door, set the house alarm, and then laid down on the couch, thinking about Alexia until he fell fast asleep.

Chapter Four: Frightener Beware...

Landon opened his eyes to the dawn of a new day and felt a heavy weight on his stomach. He looked down to see Jangers stretched out over him, chewing on one of Landon's shoes that he had retrieved from the floor.

"Well, good morning to you too, Jangers."

Jangers jumped up and joyfully licked Landon's face. He smiled, pushed the excited pup off, and stretched up from the couch. Starting his morning routine, Landon walked over to the window and placed his hand against the glass, ate breakfast with his parents, and then met Jake outside. Jake informed Landon that he had conducted a perimeter check around his house to ensure there wasn't somebody waiting for him - mostly because he believed that 'somebody' would be Roger.

As they approached the bus stop, they saw Nate and Kumar picking on one of the younger kids on their block named Johnny. Johnny was in the sixth grade and was a small and shy boy that apparently wasn't good with confrontation at all. Nate and Kumar relished in their cruelty as they taunted him by throwing his backpack back and forth over the boy's head.

"Come on, tiny. JUMP!" Kumar laughed.

Landon's blood started to boil and Jake could see by the look in his eyes that he was not going to let this continue. He approached the boys and as Nate tossed Johnny's backpack up into the air. Landon jumped in front of Kumar and intercepted the bag and then handed it back to Johnny.

"Don't you guys ever get tired of being jerks?" Landon asked rhetorically.

"Don't you ever get tired of being a dork?" Nate replied.

"Yeah, don't you ever get tired of being a dork?" Kumar repeated as he pushed

Landon.

"Shut up fat ass," shouted a whiney voice from behind them.

Roger was walking up to the bus stop with his broken hand in a cast and a mean stare in his eyes. Jake's clenched his jaw and balled his fists in preparation for another fight.

"Let's just walk, man," Jake whispered from the side of his mouth.

Landon shook his head in disagreement and faced Roger.

"So, new guy thinks he's all big and bad now. I will give you one chance to beg, otherwise, you're a dead man." Roger sneered.

Landon lowered his chin, keeping both eyes fixed on Roger.

"Okay, Roger. You win." Landon replied.

Roger smirked and raised his nose to imply that he was better than Landon while Jake stood with a look of shock plastered across his face. Landon smiled over at Jake and then yelled out in the most obnoxious voice he could.

"Roger, please! Please stop..." he paused briefly.

"Please stop avoiding the shower. And, brush yo nasty, stank-ass teeth too. You stink!"

Roger swung an angry fist at Landon's face but he dodged it and pushed Roger over by his face making him fall back onto his butt.

"Let's go!" Jake shouted as he pulled Landon away.

The boys took off in a sprint and kept running until they saw Roger and his goons give up the chase.

"Man, you must have a death wish!" Jake said heavily, in between panting breaths.

"HA! Just can't stand bullies!" Landon replied as he too caught his breath.

"I hear you on that one," said Jake as he shoved Landon to make him walk.

Landon and Jake finally made it to school and found their way to the door of their homeroom class. Kids started to pour into their seats as the boys waited for Alexia to show up and then as the last bell rang Mr. Brevander forced the three of them into the classroom and angrily shut the door behind them.

"Quiet down! Quiet down! I have to take accountability!" Mr. Brevander ordered.

As he took roll call Mr. Brevander was suddenly interrupted by Mrs. Gonzalez's voice echoing over the school's PA system.

"Good morning, Today's class schedule has been canceled," said Mrs. Gonzalez.

Anyone that had been near or passing by outside could hear the entire school erupt with cheer.

"All of your parents and legal guardians have been attempted to be notified to come and get you. Those of you whose parents and guardians we could not reach will stay here in the auditorium until we can have them come and pick you up. School will resume tomorrow at our normal time." said Mrs. Gonzalez, taking a moment to pause before she continued.

"I have one last announcement. It's a bit unsettling. As of late last night, one of our students has been reported 'missing'. Due to this, a community meeting has been called and this is the reason school has been canceled for the rest of the day. So, again, everyone will report to the auditorium and will be released as soon as their parents or legal guardians sign them out. That is all. Teachers tend to your students. Thank you." Mrs. Gonzalez finished in a stern but shaken voice.

The announcement ended, and the students were brought to the auditorium as instructed. Landon felt a heavy concern caving his chest as he, Jake and Alexia walked silently with their heads down. They sat down in the back rows of the auditorium, quietly waiting as a dull roar began to rise around them.

"Something bad is happening." Alexia whispered to Landon and Jake.

Landon and Jake nodded in agreement. Landon stared off as he envisioned the monster from his dreams and its flickering green eyes lurking in the darkness behind the dim light of the street lamps that lined their neighborhood. Jake nudged Landon, causing him to snap to as he pointed towards Landon's mother who had just entered the auditorium.

"Bro, your Mom's here," Jake whispered.

Landon got up and turned to Alexia and Jake and said his goodbyes then walked down towards her and Mr. Brevander. Landon's mother was talking to Mr. Brevander but quickly silenced their conversation as Landon approached.

"Mr. Brary, would you be so kind as to get Miss Sepulveda and Mr. Jackson? They will be leaving with you." Mr. Brevander said in an almost nice tone.

"Yes, sir!" Landon happily replied.

Landon quickly turned back and waved his hands over his head, calling out for Jake and Alexia to come over to him. Alexia and Jake picked up their belongings and ran down to Landon, who informed them they were all leaving together. As they walked towards the door, Landon could see Roger leaning by the exit doors, staring at him with a smug look on his face.

"Do you have all your things?" Moira asked, but before Landon could respond, Roger replied instead.

"Yes Ma'am, I do."

"He's coming with us?" Landon asked, pointing at Roger.

"Yes. Alexia, Jake, and Roger will stay with you at our home until their parents, along with your father and I, return from the community meeting tonight." Moira replied.

Alexia watched as Landon's face instantly turned from happy to upset at the news his mother had just shared with him. Moira didn't seem to notice and instead asked,

"Is there any station on the radio you kid's like? I'm pretty sure you don't want to listen to my music."

"Depends. You got any Wu-Tang, Homeroom 4 Sound Students, or maybe some of that sweet Bassnectar?" Jake inquired curiously.

"Who is woo tang?" Alexia asked.

"They ain't nuthin' to f with." Moira replied with a grin.

"Mom!"

"Well Landon, it's true! And, no Jake, I do not have any of those artists. I've got some Joan Jett, CCR, or AC/DC."

"I dig your style, Mrs. B. We'll go Radio this time. 94.3 is my favorite rock station here in the Springs. Seriously, they are the best. Ross, Shawn, Sid, Ox, Oz, Mo… they're the best!" Jake said happily.

"Somebody's a Kilo Rocker," Alexia laughed as they piled into Moira's custom seafoam blue and white 1967 Volkswagen minibus.

The ride home was mostly silent with the exceptions of Jake singing loudly to the songs of Tool, Alice in Chains, and the Deftones while Roger explained to Moira how he broke his hand.

"Oh, it was really weird how it happened. One moment, I was at the bus stop getting ready to step onto the bus when all of a sudden, Landon drops his bag and I go falling over it, then, SNAP!" Roger said, holding his cast up for Moira to see.

"Landon! Did you at least help Roger up?"

Before he could say anything, Roger took it upon himself to answer for him instead.

"No Ma'am, he did not, but that's okay. It's not like it was his fault." Roger explained, quickly winking back at Landon and flashing him a devious grin.

Landon scowled angrily at Roger as he continued his lie.

"I have some trouble doing things now. I have to use my left hand to do stuff, but other than that it's okay," Roger continued as he waved his cast awkwardly around in the air.

"Well, if you have to write any papers for school or do any projects, Landon will be sure to help you, won't you?" Moira replied in a voice that indicated she wasn't asking.

"Yes, Ma'am."

"Oh wow, thanks! That's really nice of you, Landon. You know, I think we're going to be good friends." Roger said, reaching his hand out for Landon to shake.

Landon quickly shook Roger's hand so his mother could see. Once she was satisfied and looked away, Landon immediately crossed his arms and stared angrily out the window for the rest of the ride home, dreading the moment that he would be left at home alone with Roger.

After they arrived at Landon's house, Moira made them all some lunch and then sent them to the living room while she made phone calls to their parents and waited for Landon's father to come home.

Roger continued to act disgustingly nice, but Landon knew he was just patiently waiting for his parents to leave. The uncomfortable silence was interrupted by Landon's father opening the door and calling out to his wife,

"Moira, I'm home! Come on, honey. We have to go," Jensen yelled from the entryway of the house.

He then turned to the living room where Alexia and the boys were sitting, watching TV. Jensen then reached over and placed his hand on Landon's head, messing up his hair and causing his son to conjure a smile through the grumpy look plastered on his face.

"Hey you guys, I'm Landon's father. Guess you guys will be staying here until we all get back. Landon, you know the rules. I'm setting the alarm and locking the doors. Don't leave or open any windows, okay? Oh, and we have tons of awesome sugary snacks or fruit or whatever in the kitchen. Go nuts, just clean up or else I'll get the ax from the 'ol ball and chain," Jensen said from the side of his mouth as if Moira couldn't hear him.

"I heard that," said Moira as she quickly made her way down the stairs. "Remember, don't answer the door at all, not for anyone. You know what to do in case of an emergency. You call me or your father if you need anything, okay?"

Landon nodded and hugged both his parents. The sound of the door being shut and locked snapped the last patient nerve in his body. Landon immediately turned to Roger and asked angrily,

"What are you even doing here?"

Roger jumped up off the couch, winked at Alexia as he strutted towards Landon, and answered smugly,

"Well, you see, your momma and me... let's just say she's not getting what she needs from your old ass pop's. Said she needs a real man. And, well..."

Landon lunged and tackled Roger to the floor. He hit Landon on the side of his head with his cast and knocked him off of him. Alexia grabbed Jake and together they scrambled to pull Landon up and away from Roger. Roger laughed as he walked slowly around the living room, picking up various things and inspecting them.

"So, new guy, this is your house, huh? Not too bad. I'm a little hungry, I'll see what you got in the fridge," Roger squeaked annoyingly and then made his way to the kitchen.

Landon turned to Jake, his face beaming with rage, and pushed his way through his friends. With balled fists, Landon paced back and forth through the living room.

"What the hell were my parents thinking? Letting Roger into our house."

"Well, technically, they don't know Roger is a jerk and that you hate him. You could always try to convince Roger to go outside and then lock the door on him," Jake replied.

They all shared in a hearty laugh. But, as much as Landon enjoyed the thought of locking Roger out or even pushing him in his face out his front door, his conscience overpowered his mind with reason. He knew his dad would be disappointed and that alone was enough for him to avoid the serious consequences of those joyous thoughts. Not to mention the punishment he would surely have to endure. Somewhere in the back of his mind, there was also a tiny voice expressing some faint concern that something terrible could actually happen to Roger and he could end up missing or hurt. Landon did not want that on his conscience.

While Roger explored Landon's refrigerator, Alexia and the boys went upstairs to Landon's room to put as much distance between themselves and him as possible. They were immediately greeted by Jangers who was laying on his back with his tongue flopped out to the side of his smiling mouth, hoping for a friendly belly scratch or two.

Landon walked over to his window and stared out onto the empty street below. No one was outside. None of the kids were running and playing. Nobody was even sitting on their porches or even driving by. Just the cold autumn wind howling and scattering the crisp leaves across the yard as the sun set behind the neighborhood rooftops. It would be dark soon and Landon's mind wandered into deeply troubling thoughts of a terrible monster.

"I hope that the cops find the person responsible for all these kidnappings soon," Alexia said, attempting to distract the boys from the dark cloud Roger's presence brought into the house.

"Well, I hope they don't. Stupid kids deserve it, if, they are really missing," Roger interrupted with a loud and sudden thud at the bedroom door.

"What's that supposed to mean?" Jake retorted.

"No surprise you haven't heard, brownie? The person responsible for taking all these kids, he is a cantabile." Roger replied smugly.

"First off, you're an ignorant racist and it really is no wonder that everyone hates you. Second, a what?" Jake asked as confusion spread across his face.

"Well, first off you and everyone else can kiss my ass crack. Second, a cantable, you idiot! It's a person who eats other people..."

"You mean, a cannibal. A person who eats another human being is called a cannibal," Jake interrupted, causing Landon and Alexia to join in the laughter.

Landon turned from the window, smiling over at Jake. His eyes were watering from laughing and the dumbfounded look upon Roger's face.

"Tell me, Roger... how exactly do you know any of this is true?" Alexia asked sarcastically.

Roger flopped down on Landon's bed and paused for a moment as he stared up at the ceiling, sighing with an air of superiority.

"Well, my parents happen to know some very important people. People who know things. People who tell my dad everything and that's all you need to know, little girl," Roger scoffed as he made his way over and sat on Landon's bed.

Landon rolled his eyes and turned back to the window, just in time to catch the last rays of the sun fall behind the houses on their street. Roger picked up his feet and, without taking his shoes off, threw them onto one of the pillows and then obnoxiously stretched out on the bed.

"Ah yes, so fluffy!"

Landon turned around, grabbed Roger's feet and threw them off his pillow as hard as he could, causing him to sit up.

"Get the hell out of my room!"

Roger quickly stood up and pushed his chest into Landon's. He did not move and stared fiercely into Roger's eyes. Roger snickered, rolled his eyes, and then pushed past Landon as he walked over to his closet and admired himself in the mirror hanging off the door.

"I see, you need some alone time with your lover? Come on Alexia," Roger said, winking at Alexia and then pushed her out into the hall.

"Get off me!" Alexia commanded and shrugged him off as he pulled her downstairs.

All of the sudden, the entire house shook violently and the lights flickered. Roger and Alexia immediately grabbed the wooden handrail of the stairs, trying to keep from falling. Landon grabbed ahold of the bedpost and looked out of the window. He was looking into complete and utter darkness. He could not see a single house or the road, even the street lamps were dark. The night had swallowed the world outside of Landon's house.

The window began to crack. It looked as if the darkness was pushing in on the glass, trying to get inside. Landon grabbed Jangers and pushed Jake to the arch of his bedroom door frame. The lights got brighter and brighter each time they flickered back on.

A loud roaring wind burst through every door and darkness flooded the house. Landon could hear things crashing and breaking as the roaring wind tore through the house. The roar transformed into an ear-piercing scream that dropped all of the children to the floor.

Roger sobbed nervously, tears pouring from his eyes and a large snot bubble growing under his nose. As the house continued to shake, he started screaming in an extremely high pitch and tightly gripped the handrail with both hands. And then, just as suddenly as the house shaking began, it stopped and became disturbingly quiet. The lights stopped flickering and for a moment, all was calm. The children slowly stood up and looked around to see what had caused the house to shake.

"Earthquake?" Landon asked.

"I don't think so..." Jake answered.

Then, without warning, all the lights in the house rapidly flickered. There was a loud boom as though something huge landed downstairs. One by one the lights throughout the house exploded, sending glass and tiny embers into the darkness. The glass from each window screeched with sharp creaks and snapping cracks. There was something in the house and it was moving towards them.

"I'm okay, everything is fine. It's just an earthquake," Jake repeated softly, hugging the door frame and keeping his eyes tightly closed.

Landon looked past Roger and Alexia and watched the darkness move closer and smother the light behind them. He felt his stomach twist and his heart race. Then, as if time suddenly slowed to a crawl, the last light flickered above Alexia and Roger. It burst into a sparkling white rain of fire and glass that rained beautifully down on them.

Landon stood paralyzed, unable to move. He was trapped in a slower version of reality as Alexia and Roger were swallowed into a terrifyingly familiar thick black smoke by two rotting hands with silver claws.

Roger saw the rotten hands reaching for them and belted out a loud squeal as he shoved Alexia in front of him. The boys all watched in horror as she was wrenched into the darkness and her screams instantly became deathly silent. Then, the wretched hands shot out from the smoke and carelessly tore Roger from the handrail. Roger disappeared into the darkness, screaming and kicking. Suddenly, there was a loud crunch and he was silent.

Time immediately sped up to its normal pace and suddenly, Jake pulled Landon back into the safety of his room. As he fell backward, Landon stared into the hallway and felt his entire body tense as if he had just been struck by lightning. There, within that swelling darkness, two hauntingly familiar emerald eyes burned brightly and stared menacingly back at him.

Chapter Five: Time to Wake Up...

Jake kicked the door shut and Landon fell onto the floor.

His heart pumping vigorously as fear rushed through his veins.

Jake ran to Landon and started to pull him up, but he was locked in

the grip of terror. Something he had believed was only a

nightmare, something he thought could never truly be real,

something that had haunted Landon for as long as he could

remember was now standing at his bedroom door.

"Landon?" Jake yelled, clapping his hands in front of

Landon's face.

"This is no time to go comatose. Snap out of it, man!"

"Fire! We have to climb out." Jake yelled.

Black smoke seeped through the space from underneath

Landon's bedroom door. Jake ran to the window and tried to

push it open, but it wouldn't budge. Suddenly, the house began to

shake again and the light in Landon's room flickered off. Jake immediately turned around and saw a monstrous black cloud filling the room and ice spreading across the ceiling.

Landon, still stuck in a daze, saw the black cloud briefly shrink away when light on the ceiling came on before smashing the bulb. Landon pulled himself free from fear and ran to his closet. He threw open the door and grabbed a flashlight from one the boxes within. This was not just any flashlight. This was an LED flashlight with the light of thirty-three thousand lumens.

"Landon! What are you doing?" Jake yelled.

"Watch."

Landon flicked the flashlight on and pointed it at the cloud of smoke. It let out a terrible scream and immediately retreated into the hallway. Still shining the light, Landon moved towards the door. Jangers, who was hiding under the bed, growled as Landon inched towards the door.

"You're telling me, boy," Landon whispered.

"Don't go out there. Why would you go out there? Haven't you seen scary movies? You don't go into the dark." Jake vehemently questioned and stated.

"It's the only way out."

The light in Landon's room flickered and then came back on. The bright light even lit some of the hallway. Jake held Jangers and shook his head as Landon leaned out into the hallway. He pointed the flashlight out into the darkness, but he saw nothing. The smoke vanished.

Suddenly, a loud thump came from above. Landon jumped back and then thrust the flashlight forward into the darkness, waiting for it to attack. After a moment passed and nothing happened, he realized he was okay. Landon leaned out of his door frame and shined his flashlight down the hall.

There was another thump from above, Landon quickly shined his flashlight at the ceiling and watched as trickles of dust fell from the access panel to the attic. Inching away from his room and into the dark hallway, Landon heard yet another thump and another.

Landon stood under the access panel. Jake and Jangers watching him from the doorway. Then, just as he reached up to pull the cord his flashlight flickered. Landon turned and stared into the darkness and at the end of the hallway. It looked like it was moving. All of a sudden, the two burning green eyes appeared. His heart pounded and a lump formed in his throat. Trying not to sound frightened Landon asked,

"What are you?"

The fiery eyes stared and the darkness hissed. Landon raised his flashlight and pointed the intense ray of light at staring eyes. Black smoke and ash filled the hallway as it hissed and tried to block out the ray of light. Jake mustered his courage and ran out of the room, meeting Landon in the hallway under the attic entrance.

"Whatever that thing is… it's afraid of the light. You hear that noise? It's coming from the attic." said Landon nervously keeping the darkness at bay.

"Yeah," Jake whispered.

"You aren't thinking of going up there are you?"

"Just hold this and keep it pointed that way," said Landon, ignoring Jake's question and handing him the flashlight.

"Are you crazy? You don't even know what that is up there!"

"Alexia and Roger might be up there," Landon replied as he pulled the string to the attic door down.

"Which is why we should get the hell out of here and call the cops or… a monster hunter, or something!"

From the corner of his eye Jake saw the dark cloud inch closer and he immediately raised the light into its fiery eyes. As Jake screamed, so did the darkness as it retreated back to the end of the hallway. Landon jumped up and grabbed ahold of the cord, pulled it down, and unfolded the ladder. But, before climbing up, Landon paused. Then, turned back to Jake and asked,

"Wait… where is Jangers?"

"Are you kidding?" Jake replied sarcastically.

"Jake!"

"He ran down the stairs and out the front door. Just like we should!" Jake answered, shaking his head in disbelief.

"I am going up there. You can stay down here or run if you like, but I am going."

Jake widened his eyes and stretched his arms as far out in front of him as he possibly could, pointing the high-powered beam directly into the darkness at the end of the hall. The house echoed with furious screams and terrifying howls of the monster. Landon cautiously climbed up into the attic with Jake below urging him to go faster.

Landon took in a deep breath and raced up the rest of the ladder. He looked around, but he couldn't see anything. The attic was pitch black. Landon turned and whispered down to Jake,

"Your turn,"

Jake took in a deep breath and quickly psyched himself up. Then he tossed the light up to Landon and scrambled up the ladder. As soon as Jake turned the flashlight away the black smoke screamed and raced towards the ladder with two rotting hands reaching out to grab his legs.

Landon pulled Jake up into the attic and locked the door just as the ladder exploded below. Jake grabbed the flashlight and shined it around the attic. There was no trace of smoke or green eyes. For the moment they were both safe and stuck.

Landon and Jake ran from the door and hid in a corner of attic behind a few dusty trunks and weathered boxes. From there they could see the attic door swelling as the darkness below clawed and pounded to get in.

"Great! Now we have nowhere to go!" Jake whispered sarcastically.

"Calm down. There is a window just over there. Once we find Alexia and Roger we will get out of here."

"Calm down? Calm down? If there ever was a moment to not be calm, this is it! You calm down," Jake scoffed.

"Take the flashlight and keep it pointed at that door. I will look for Alexia and Roger," Landon whispered as he handed the light over to Jake.

"You are crazy. I knew it. I knew it!"

"Just keep that thing from coming in here until I get back." Landon said, pointing at the attic door.

Landon maneuvered around scattered boxes and old furniture, past a rickety desk and a heavily cobwebbed chair as he searched the attic. He slowly made his way through the darkness, cautiously searching for Alexia and Roger. All of a sudden, there was another loud thump and this time it came from behind a stack boxes in a dark corner in front of Landon.

"Alexia?"

Landon peered over the boxes and into the corner. He saw something lying on the floor, under a large oval stand-up mirror. Another loud thump broke through the silence and Landon could see it was coming from whatever was under the mirror. He moved around the boxes and quietly made his way closer until he could see clearly. Somebody was caught beneath the mirror.

"Roger?" Landon asked hesitantly.

"Jake, come here! I think I found Roger."

Jake reluctantly placed the light on top of one of the dusty trunks in a position to shine on the attic door and then ran over to Landon. Together, they reached down and positioned themselves to lift the mirror.

"One, two, three..." Landon said as the two boys lifted the heavy mirror.

Once they had lifted it upright, they immediately discovered someone who was definitely not Roger.

"Jake get the flashlight!"

Before Jake could move, the figure stood up and instantly smashed its head straight into the ceiling.

"OW!" it screamed in a frightening voice.

Landon and Jake stumbled over each other as they tried to back away to safety. Whoever this was in front of them was extremely tall and had to hunch over to fit in the attic. As the boys scrambled to their feet, two long hands with twisted fingers reached out for them both.

"Aw, man! I'm totally gonna die tonight!" Jake whimpered.

At that moment, the attic door burst open, and the dark smoke raced inside, screaming as it reached out and smashed the flashlight. The strange tall figure grabbed both the boys and once more, time slowed to a crawl.

Landon felt his body become weightless as the smoke stretched its rotten hands out towards him. Fear paralyzed him and set his veins on fire, causing his heart to beat madly. As he fell backwards, dazzling and colorful lights began to spiral all around him. It looked like he was falling down into a spiraling neon vortex.

Suddenly, a brilliant white flash of light blinded Landon and he felt his body smash onto something hard. His vision blurred and his body was unresponsive to his command to move it. He could feel his eyelids become heavy and his brain shutting down. The last thing he heard before his sight became black and he passed out was a faint voice asking,

"Which one is he?"

Chapter Six: Out in the Dark...

Roger's body shook violently. The cold bite of fear gnawed on his every nerve. His vision was as black as night. He could see nothing around him, not even his own hands that he frantically waved in front of his face. He quickly realized his body was sliding across the wet ground. Something was dragging him.

"Where am I?" he whimpered.

Whatever was dragging him stopped. Suddenly, Roger was thrown high up into the air and was just as quickly slammed back down onto the frigid ground. He writhed in pain as he stretched out into the darkness surrounding him. His eyes wide as he desperately sought to find a way out. Roger could feel the wind of whatever just threw him, circling around him. It stopped briefly and then a thin and boney hand violently grasped the top of his head.

Instantly, he was yanked out of the darkness and was hanging high in the chilling night air by his head. Five knife-like fingers pierced into his skin. Pain rippled through his entire body and his eyes filled with blood. Roger screamed and a second rotten hand grabbed his face. A putrid smell of decay stained his nostrils and filled his lungs, making him gag.

"Please..." he choked.

"Please, stop."

Then, like a rag doll, he was quickly brought face to face with his captor. Roger's eyes widened as blood and tears streamed down his face. Holding him was a towering monster with several long and sharp black steel blades protruding from the skin of its skeletal head like a painful crown. Its skeletal face was covered in a white skin that looked like it had been stretched too tightly over a fierce looking skull with no muscle.

Deep within the black wells of its eye sockets burned a pair of fiery green eyes staring wildly at Roger. Below its black nasal cavity, long razor-sharp silver teeth salivated. It had no lips. Instead, the skin buried into the bone just above its rotting gum line, exposing its gnashing teeth.

The nightmarish monster's body was wrapped in a suffocating burnt armor and black leather. Gaps, between the metal and leather glowed with red hot embers, like that of burning coal. Sharp and fractured bits of bone pierced through the armor and protruded from its spine, knees, and elbows.

The monster pulled Roger close and slashed at his chest with its silver claws. When he howled in agony, it widely stretched opened its jaws and started sucking in all the air around him. He felt something being pulled out of him from deep within the bones of his body. A faint gray mist rose from his skin and was sucked into the monster's mouth.

"What are you?" Roger cried.

The monster's emerald eyes flickered menacingly and then, without mercy, Roger was thrown high into the air and slammed viciously back down onto the ground. The fall broke both of his legs and knocked him unconscious.

Smoke and ash billowed out from the monster's spine and wrapped around Roger like a cocoon. Then, as though nothing happened, it turned back into the night and continued dragging

Roger's body into darkness.

Chapter Seven: The Land of Nod...

"He's waking up... "

Landon opened his eyes and heard footsteps quickly

shuffling across a wooden floor towards him. He could feel

someone helping him from off the floor and up onto his feet. His

head rushed with stars that danced into his eyes, threatening to

black out his sight completely, but faded quickly as he stood up.

Feeling dizzy and dazed, Landon opened his eyes as wide as he

could, clearing out the blurriness, and then surveyed his

surroundings.

He was in a circular room with the walls draped in tattered

burgundy curtains. Above him, hanging from a cone-shaped

vaulted ceiling, hung a wrought iron chandelier adorned with many

melting candles. Below the chandelier, a large black and white

spiral rug that seemed purposefully positioned underneath to catch

all of the dripping wax.

A long bed with crooked iron posts sat a few feet from him. It was layered in patchwork quilts and giant overstuffed pillows. Standing across from the bed was a tall oval mirror with a beautiful and elegant silver frame. Its surface rippling softly with various colors. Suddenly, an unsettling voice came from behind Landon's and said,

"Hello Landon. My name is Simon Hush."

The sound of the voice sent a slight shiver down Landon's spine. It sounded as though three people had just spoken to him simultaneously screeching, whispering, and talking all at the same time. Landon slowly turned around and discovered an extremely tall and frightening figure. The strangeness of his appearance startled Landon and caused him to immediately back away.

Simon was over nine feet tall and wore a tattered red and green striped turtleneck sweater that was ripped and torn at every opening, brown corduroy pants with a single red patch on the left knee, and a very large pair of worn out, dark brown boots that were curled up at the tips like the shoes the elves wear. At the ends of each tattered sleeve were long thin hands with sharp and splintering vine-like fingers protruding out from bandaged palms.

Resting above the opening of the ripped-up turtleneck collar, sat Simon's strange head. Landon could not see a face because it was completely wrapped in dirty bandages. Simon's face looked like a mummy that had a single bronzed tube with a red lens, protruding about an inch out from within the wrappings, covering the right eye. His thick black hair was wildly long and seemed to defy gravity.

As Landon scanned the room and searched for an exit, Simon lowered his face down to his and then calmly said,

"Landon, do not be afraid."

Even though the sound of Simon's voice was frightening, Landon believed there was no need to be afraid and felt his need to flee transition into curiosity. Still cautious, he put a little distance between them and then boldly asked,

"Where are we? What the hell was that thing? And, what are you?"

"We are in Nod, that was Vyle, and I am a Frightener," Simon answered as he reached down and happily shook Landon's hand.

Simon didn't wait for Landon to speak as he could easily see the confusion on his face. Rather, he continued trying to explain what he knew to most would be unimaginable. Simon pointed a long finger at the bed and spoke up a little louder,

"And, that little guy under my bed is, Jeckles."

Suddenly, a bright green ball - much larger than a basketball - rolled out from underneath the crooked bed. Jeckles paused for a minute and then bounced high up into the air. Red and white stripped arms with white gloves and legs with shiny black shoes popped out of him as he landed. Jeckles interlocked his then four-fingered hands, cracked them, and then opened his beady little black eyes. Jeckles bowed and quickly retrieved a top hat and a monocle. Landon could not figure out where he got them because Jeckles wasn't wearing any clothes. Jeckles wiggled his extremely tiny nose and smiled at Landon as a red licorice cane magically appeared in his hand.

"Hello," Jeckles said in a comforting English voice, winking at Landon and hopping up onto Simon's bed.

Landon could not believe his eyes and for a moment, he considered the possibility that he may have hit his head or something. The moment passed when Landon touched his shoulder and felt a dull pain run through his arm. Verifying that, in fact, this was all real.

"What did you mean by, frightener, and where did that Vyle thing go?" Landon asked nervously.

"You do not need to worry. Vyle cannot get you here. This Endindrium is enchanted and only I know the way through."

"Endindrium?" Landon questioned.

"Yes, this is an Endindrium, only this one has been made special. Only I know the way through the labyrinth between. If you don't know which way to go, this one will spit you out to the edges of Nod. Someone very dear to us made this one for me."

"As for what an Endindrium is, it's a passageway that creates a bridge from our world to yours." Simon explained as he pointed to a rippling mirror elegantly wrapped in a silver frame, standing across from the bed.

"And, you are a Frightener?"

"Yes, but first, I was a Dreamer. Your Dreamer to be more specific. On Earth, I would be known as your imaginary friend."

"Do we look imaginary to you?" Jeckles huffed.

"When a child is born on Earth, a Dreamer is also born here in Nod. A Dreamer is a being as unique as a star, as creative as a galaxy, and like you, a beautiful perspective within this fabric of existence. Dreamers help children open the doors to confidence, strength, and self-love by amplifying the power of their imaginations," Simon continued.

He reached one long arm behind the nearby curtain and pulled down on a long golden rope. The tattered curtain walls were slowly drawn up and disappeared into the ceiling. Landon took a look around and saw that there were no walls, just a single window that wrapped around the entire room, held together by spiraling wrought iron braces.

"Do you see that bright sliver of light stretching up into the sky far out in the distance? That is where I come from. It is called, Reflection City."

Landon looked out the window and saw that he was inside some kind of crooked wooden tower, perched high over an ocean of moving sand dunes, swaying dangerously over the crumbling edge of a thin cliff. He turned his sight to the sliver of light and traced it up to a night sky, powdered with glowing clouds and glittering stars. Landon could even see a few tiny planets and what looked like a tiny neon spaceship zig-zagging around one of them.

Simon reached into his pocket and retrieved a silver ring. He then stretched his arm out and dropped it into Landon's open hand. The stone in Simon's ring wasn't red, nor was it clear. Instead, it was as black as night.

"When a Dreamer is born, they are given a ring. The ring is called a, Ki. Each Ki is created, tuned, and individually synchronized to the harmony of a child's heartbeat by Sentinel. Then, the moment a child's heart calls to their Dreamer, that Dreamer's ring will sing and the stone will change from red to clear. When that happens, a Dreamer can then unlock the Endindriums and cross over to Earth. I used to go to the center of Reflection City to a place called, The Fountain of Dreams. It's a magnificent crystal tower. It is place where Dreamers are born. Where I was born. Pouring from the tip of tower, down into specially carved channels on the ground, flows the magical waters of creation connected to the Root. These magical waters flow down the walls of The Fountain of Dreams, through special channels carved out by the Sandmen, and power the thousands of rings of Endindriums. It was my favorite place to go when I was a Dreamer. I used to sit there for hours… waiting and dreaming," Simon said as he traced a twisted finger over the mirror's silver frame, pausing to quietly reflect on the memory.

"What happened next?"

"I broke a rule."

"Two," said Jeckles.

"A Dreamer shall not enter an Endindrium until the day their child's heart opens the way. And, a Dreamer shall not bring a child into Nod."

"I'll never forget that night. Almost twelve years ago on December fifteenth I came into your world and into your life. It was late at night and I decided to go to watch the waterfall. I was there for a while, just staring off. When all of a sudden, right in front of me, an Endindrium opened up."

"I remember watching it ripple and waiting for someone to come out, but none ever did. I knew, deep down, I knew I shouldn't enter it. But, I did. I did it knowing that something bad could happen and I did it anyway. I didn't care about the rules and all I could think was this might be my only chance."

"So, I walked in and was transported into your room. You were only a baby then, but it was like you already knew me. You smiled and giggled, a lot. I remember the feeling of joy fill my entire being. It was quickly becoming the happiest day of my life. But, I did not arrive alone. I brought a terrible darkness with me. I wanted so desperately to meet you that when I entered the

126

Endindrium without your permission, I ripped a Nightmare from its dark pit and brought it with me."

Landon felt a cold chill run up his spine and trickle down into his veins. Fiery green eyes flashed into his thoughts. His lungs began to feel thin and his breathing turned shallow. A cold sweat leaked from his pores at the thought of a thick black smoke choking him. Landon sat nervously on the edge of his own vessel, riding the wave of anxiety. Taking in mindfully deep breaths, he quickly steered himself into calmer state as Simon continued.

"When a Dreamer is born, so is something else... a Nightmare. They are wretched creatures that live in underbelly of Nod. In a pit of darkness called, Nyx."

"They are parasitic things that feed on fear. They do this by entering a child's dream and infecting it with terror. It changes the dream and when the child becomes afraid the Nightmare feeds off of their fear. Eventually, children learn how to fight back against Nightmares within the safety of their dreams and over time become less afraid. Your Nightmare followed me through the Endindrium that night. His name is Vyle."

"Vyle? How did you bring him to my world?" Landon asked, still breathing deeply.

"When a Dreamer enters an Endindrium before their Ki is ready, it changes the energy, frequency, and vibrations that allows for them to travel safely between worlds. The Endindrium aligns that particular child's imaginative energies and opens the passageway to Nyx."

"When I entered, I opened a portal in Nyx that pulled Vyle into that space between our worlds and led him into your room. You were so afraid. I watched him feed on your fear. It was real, pure, and raw. I can still hear your cries. I tried to stop him, but he was so strong. When Vyle touched me, my whole body felt like it was on fire. Somewhere in a whirlwind of smoke he... he changed me."

"Ever since that night, all the Endindriums in Nod have been enchanted..." Jeckles quietly added.

"I remember that night, almost every night, in my dreams. It's always felt real," Landon said softly.

As the memory came to a conclusion, Landon turned and looked back out of the window, down onto the rolling waves of sand. Suddenly, he remembered that he was not the only one to have come to Nod and shouted,

"Jake! Where is Jake?"

"Well?" Simon asked Jeckles.

"Well..." Jeckles replied, pausing as he backed away from Landon.

"He kind of freaked out a little and wouldn't calm down. So..." Jeckles continued, starring down at the rug and sweeping a foot back and forth in front of him.

"I found him downstairs and he was screaming at me. I got scared and sort of pushed... I locked him in a room next to the stairs."

"You what? Where? Take me to him, now!" Landon screamed.

Simon instantly shot up out of his chair and quickly threw the rug and Jeckles aside. Underneath was a large round door in the wooden floor. Simon pulled up on a silver latch and threw the door wide open. Below was a spiraling staircase of twisted wrought iron and wooden steps that were at least ten stories high.

"Off we go," Jeckles said as he pushed Landon down the onto the first step.

Suddenly, Landon felt his body sliding down the spiraling staircase. It transformed into a slide and in seconds, he had reached the bottom. Landon landed gently on a giant purple pillow with Simon and Jeckles following right behind him. Landon rolled out of the way just as they shot out onto the pillow. Simon jumped up and spread his long arms out and shouted with delight,

"Let's do that again!"

Landon immediately noticed a door and quickly opened it. It led to Simon's living room, where he found a magnificent stone fireplace, a couple of brown wingback armchairs, and crooked bookshelf littered with novels. Landon raced through the living room and into a cozy kitchen. There wasn't much in it besides a sink, a tall table with four different chairs, and a slightly hunched over refrigerator that Landon could have sworn he heard snoring as he ran by. He threw open a tall, red door from and found a long hallway. There were ten different doors on each side of the hall and one giant door at the end. Landon turned to Jeckles and asked impatiently,

"Well, which one is he in?"

Jeckles crossed his arms and placed one hand under what must have been his chin, quietly thinking to himself as he pointed to various doors until finally deciding on one.

"Try that one."

"Are you telling me you don't know?"

"It happened so fast. I... I forgot where I put him, mate. I'm sorry," Jeckles said shamefully before tucking his body into a ball and rolling back into the living room where he hid under one of the armchairs.

Landon ran to the door Jeckles had pointed out and reached for the door handle. Only there wasn't a handle - instead, there was a golden hand.

"Don't worry about him. He's just sensitive. He means well and really didn't mean to lose your friend," said Simon as Landon inspected the door.

"How do I open this door?"

Simon bent down and examined it, then shrugged his wide shoulders and replied,

"I don't know."

"You don't know?" Landon yelled angrily.

Simon crossed his arms and stared away from Landon showing him he did not appreciate Landon's attitude.

"It's not nice to yell. Besides, I have never seen any of these doors, except that one at the end, until you got here," Simon responded with a resentful tone.

"Then how did they get here?"

"That's a good question."

"What if it's true and he can pretend?" Jeckles whispered, peeking from behind the kitchen door.

"Pretend? You mean like playing?"

"As in using your imagination to make something real or even more, create a reality!" answered Jeckles excitedly.

"Pretend you can open the door," Simon said curiously, rubbing a finger under his bandaged chin.

Landon let out a frustrated sigh and returned to the door, trying to turn the hand. Suddenly, a secret handshake he used to do with a few friends from his old school came to mind. Before he knew it, Landon and the golden hand were performing the secret handshake. The hand responded to every grasp, bump, and finger snap then immediately opened. Instantly, Jake tumbled out and landed right on his face. Jake quickly scrambled back up to his feet and shouted,

"Get off me! Get off me! who wants some? I'll kill…"

"It is true! They… he can pretend!" Jeckles interrupted.

Landon felt a sudden explosion of pain burst in his head. He became light-headed and fell against the wall for a moment until the pain subsided. As the dizziness wore off, and the stars cleared his vision, Landon turned to find Jake with his fists balled and ready to swing at Simon.

"Jake, it's okay. That's Simon and Jeckles. We are safe. We're in a place called Nod. I'm not too sure of anything else though."

After calming Jake down, they all entered Simon's kitchen and sat down at the giant table. Everything was very tall, just like Simon. As Landon climbed up onto a chair, he saw the pale blue refrigerator hunched over on the floor. It was indeed snoring. He chuckled, turned to Jake, and pointed out the snoring refrigerator. Jake's eyes widened in disbelief as he sat down next to Landon and Simon.

"Landon, you can pretend," Jeckles said as he stood in awe.

"So, everybody can pretend?" Landon scoffed.

"No, not everyone can. Especially, not here in Nod. It's something special. Only a few Dreamers can and even then, it requires an immense amount of focus to do what you did with the door so effortlessly. Would've drained a Dreamer, I bet. All except…"

"You and your stories," Simon interrupted Jeckles.

"Where there's smoke, mate. Besides, they may be true. Remember when I said Simon broke two rules?"

"Yeah," Landon answered.

"Well, the reason for the second rule is because of what you just did! To put it simply, a child in Nod is dangerous because of your abilities to pretend. We were warned that a child could literally change our entire world!"

"Simon, was that Vyle who was after us at the house?" Landon asked.

"Yes."

"Ever since that night, I have had this foggy connection to him. I think all Nightmares have a connection to each other, especially to Vyle," Simon said shaking his head.

Simon stared down at Landon and with a low voice he explained in great detail the accounts of what had happened after he returned from Landon's room.

"That night, when he fed off of you, he changed me... into this. After that, everything became a blur. I remember falling back to Nod and a bright light. Jeckles and Sentinel found me unconscious next to the Endindrium. All the Dreamers there were scared except..."

"Except me! Of course, Sentinel already knew. They know EVERYTHING!" Jeckles delightfully interjected.

"Sentinel?" Jake asked.

"Yeah, mate. Deity created them. She runs the show around Nod. Never met her myself, but I hear she is as bright as the sun. Anyway, there are these Dreamers that have been chosen to protect their city and the Endindriums. Every city has 'em and they are all connected to each other. The call themselves Sentinel."

"Deity created them after the first Nightmare attack on a glimmering city wonder called, Del Toro. It was a massacre. Only two survived to tell what happened. Absolutely, utterly, horrifying. Most call it, Ciudad De Pesadillas, now. Anyway, Sentinel knew what Simon had done and took him to the tower. Silver jerks didn't even let me go with him," Jeckles explained.

"I don't remember anything except waking up, strapped to a table. They had never seen anything like me… half Dreamer, half Nightmare. Frightener is what they called me and what they told all of Nod before they banished me, sent me here. Said it was to protect the city, to protect me," said Simon.

"They banished Simon, because they believed he would attract Nightmares. They were wrong. Nightmare attacks happened all over Nod." said Jeckles as he crossed his candy cane arms and stuck his tiny nose up in the air.

"That night… Vyle didn't just feed on your fear, Landon. I think he fed on your soul. When he returned, he had changed too. Vyle became incredibly powerful and even more terrifying. He crowned himself Lord Vyle, King of all Nightmares, and ruler of Nyx."

"After he returned, he and his Nightmare hordes attacked Nod relentlessly, seeking to gain control of the Endindriums and entrance back into your world. After Del Toro, Dreamers discovered the Nightmares infectious abilities and certain measures were taken. The fight still continues to stop Vyle," Simon answered.

"But, Vyle found a way back in our world. He found me," Landon exclaimed.

"I suspect Vyle has been searching for ways to get back into your world. Since that night, I have been able to feel his insatiable hunger grow. It gnaws at him," said Simon eerily as he walked out of the kitchen and over to the fireplace.

He knelt down and started a purple fire from his hands. Simon stared deeply into it, watching the flames dance and grow as Landon, Jake, and Jeckles followed him into the living room.

"The last sun is setting do you feel them?" Jeckles asked.

Simon stood still and lifted his head all the way to the ceiling. He raised both of his arms up from his sides and stretched out his long and twisted fingers. To Landon, Simon looked a lot like a scarecrow. Next, he slowly spun around, feeling the air around them. After a few circles, Simon dropped his arms and answered,

"None that are strong enough to matter. We are safe for now."

Jeckles jumped off the chair and motioned for everyone to follow him down the hallway. Landon and Simon followed, but Jake did not move. Instead, he stayed seated with a scowl on his face and his arms crossed.

"Jake what are you doing?" Landon asked.

"Yeah right, I am not going anywhere that little green booger leads me!"

Jeckles body slumped a little and tears began welling in his eyes. Landon walked over to Jake and pushed him towards the hallway,

"Come on, ya big baby! Jeckles didn't mean to put you in a closet. He didn't even know it was one. Besides, it won't happen again, right mate?"

Jeckles delightfully nodded his round body in agreement and dried his eyes with a red handkerchief that, again, was seemingly pulled out of nowhere.

"See, now let's go," said Landon, continuing to nudge Jake forward into the hallway.

"So, we can either climb the stairs all the way back up to Simon's room or we could try one of these doors. Either way, we are staying here tonight and leaving at the first sun rise. It will be safer to leave then," Jeckles said to Simon and then turned to Landon.

"Leave? Where are we going?" Landon asked.

"To Reflection City," Simon answered.

"I thought that you were banished?" Jake asked.

"I don't follow the rules."

"That's not funny. Now either pick a door or let's get to climbing," said Jeckles, impatiently tapping his foot.

"Pick a door," said both boys simultaneously.

Landon walked down the hall and approached a large round wooden door. He gently placed his hands upon its smooth surface and breathed in deeply. Keeping his hands on the door, Landon stood with his eyes closed, trying to imagine the door opening. Instantly he felt it budge. Landon opened his eyes and pushed the door open wide enough to peek his head inside. There was nothing behind the door but darkness.

"Hello?" Landon shouted, hearing his voice trail off into the empty abyss.

"What Are you doing?" Jake asked as Landon turned back to the hall and closed the door.

"I am trying to pretend,"

"Try imagining the room. See if that works," said Simon.

"Pretend? Try imagining the room?" Jake questioned sarcastically.

"I think, in this world, pretending is equal to magic. Earlier, when you were locked in the closet. The doorknob was a golden hand. Simon said he didn't know how to unlock it. I remembered this secret handshake I used to do. Then, I pretended the hand was real and did the shake. Next thing you know, the door opened."

"Wait, so you're saying we can make anything we can imagine here?" Jake asked excitedly.

"I think so," Landon answered.

Landon placed both of his hands once more upon the door and closed his eyes. He pictured a room with four beds with giant pillows and thick blankets. Once he felt satisfied with the image, he opened his eyes. As Landon pushed the door open, his head instantly filled with pain and fell against the wall.

"Are you okay?" asked Simon.

Landon shook his head and waited for his vision to clear before responding to Simon.

"Yeah, I think so. That's the second time that has happened. What is that?"

I am not sure, Simon answered, shrugging his shoulders.

The pain lingered a little longer than before, but eventually receded. Landon reached up and then pushed the door open. The room was still dark, but the light from the hallway cut through the darkness enough that it allowed them to see the room was enormous. There were no windows, no lights, and sitting in a small circle a few feet from the door was a ring of tiny beds no bigger than that of Landon's foot. Everyone immediately burst into laughter.

"Great imagination, Landon," chuckled Jake.

"Then, let's see you do better, Maynard."

"Maynard? Hell yeah! That is quiet an imagination," Jake grinned.

"It wasn't meant to be a compliment."

"Whatever. Get ready to call me, badass." said Jake confidently as he folded his hands together, interlocked his fingers, and then popped all of his knuckles.

"Show me what you got!"

Jake closed the door, placed his hands upon its surface, and closed his eyes. He began concentrating as hard as he could, picturing a luxurious hotel room he stayed in on vacation with his family. Like Landon, once he felt satisfied with the image, he peeked inside and saw nothing changed. Jake closed the door, took in a deep breath, and tried focusing even harder. Then, releasing all the trapped air from his lungs, Jake opened his eyes and pushed the door open. Still, nothing changed. The room was exactly the same.

"I got nothing," Jake exclaimed feeling defeated.

Suddenly, a sharp pain shot through Jake's head. He stumbled and fell onto the floor. Landon dropped down next to him and waited it out. Once Jake opened his eyes, Landon helped him back up onto his feet.

"That really hurt! What was that all about?" Jake asked Landon, his head lightly throbbing.

"I don't know, but it goes away."

Landon returned to the door and tried again. He specifically focused on the beds being larger. His intensity caused him to push the door slightly open. Enough for Jake, Simon, and Jeckles to see four beds growing to an unbelievably gigantic size.

"Landon, stop! That's enough," Jake yelled, interrupting Landon's focus.

With a giant exhale, Landon opened his eyes and waited for his vision to clear. Suddenly, another bolt of searing pain stabbed at the core of his brain like a million brain freezes. He immediately fell to the ground, grabbed his head, and screamed. Jake reached down and tried to help but he didn't know what to do. So, he just waited by Landon, watching him writhe in pain until it passed. Then, he helped Landon back up onto his feet and into the room.

Landon looked up at an enormous bed towering in front of him. Simon reached down and, one by one, helped them up onto the ledge of the bed frame. Then, they climbed up to the sheets to the top of the humongous mattress. Simon reached down to Jeckles, but he declined by shaking his round body. He curled into a ball, speedily rolled himself up the post, and flew high up into the air over the giant bed. Jeckles then popped himself open and slowly floated down like a feather onto one of the pillows.

"Show off," whispered Jake.

Simon, being so tall, climbed up effortlessly after them. Suddenly, Jeckles repeatedly slammed himself next to Jake and after a few bounces, he laid down. In seconds, Jeckles was fast asleep and snoring loudly. Jake sat there looking at Landon dumbfound. Got up and then walked to the opposite end of the bed, far away from Jeckles. After finding a comfortable spot, Jake laid down and dozed off.

Landon sat on the edge of the mattress, staring out into the dark room. He closed his eyes and pictured tiny stars. Simon sat down next to him and watched in wonder as small flickers of glowing light began to sparkle above. Landon felt a small pinch of pain, then opened his eyes and looked up to the stars he created. They sat quietly admiring glittering stars together for a while. Neither one feeling the need to fill the air with words. Then, Landon stretched up, smiled sleepily at Simon, and made his way to the other pillow and drifted off into a dream.

Simon did not move. He stayed seated at the edge of the bed, watching the stars dance above him. Being half Nightmare, sleep left his company long ago.

Chapter Eight: A World of Nightmares...

The sounds of clanking metal drifted through Roger's ears. His head was heavy and his body ached with pain. He reached up and rubbed the blur from his eyes. Roger's wrists and neck were chained to a wet stone wall and he could see that he was locked in a dark dungeon. Bolted along the stone walls, green flames danced upon torches and reflected off rippling puddles collecting water from the ceiling. The air was saturated with the overpowering smells of mildew and something rotting. The putrid smell climbed up Roger's nostrils, down the back of his throat, and made him throw up.

The wind cut through the dungeon and Roger could hear something rustling near him. He squinted his eyes and searched the darkness, trying to see where the sound emanated. There was somebody sitting underneath one of the flickering torches. The wind calmed, and the flame grew a little brighter. There, chained to the wall and covered in rags, was a pale skeleton. Again, the wind came and rattled its bones.

Roger sat up and immediately felt a piercing pain shoot up through his spine from his broken legs. His screams rang through the darkness and echoed off the wet stone walls. Scared and in agonizing pain, he cried,

"Help!"

"Be quiet," urged a familiar voice.

Roger could hear someone shuffling towards him and the sounds of metal dragging across the floor. He could see a slight outline of a small person crawling towards him. He tried to keep from crying but could not keep from letting muffled pain filled sobs escape his mouth.

"Who's there?" he whimpered.

"It's me, Alexia."

"Alexia?" Roger said somewhat relieved.

"You have to stay quiet," said Alexia, moving into the dim green light so Roger could see her.

Alexia's face had aged tremendously. Her eyes were sunken in and her hair had become thin and gray. She looked old and malnourished.

"Where... where are we?" Roger struggled to ask, choking back the pain.

"I don't know, but you have to be quiet!"

"What is that?" Roger asked. Looking over at the skeleton rattling next to him.

Alexia did not answer. Instead, she turned her head to listen. Roger stopped talking and listened as well. Suddenly, there was a loud bang above their heads. Alexia scrambled back into the shadows and whispered,

"It's coming!"

Roger could hear the creaking of a metal door opening. The flames dulled and one by one, died out until the dungeon was pitch black. The dripping ceiling became frozen as ice creeped along the walls toward Roger. He held his breath and tried desperately not to make a sound.

"Child," said a sinister voice.

White sparks burst above Roger's head and rained down onto him as a rotting hand dragged its sharp claws across the wall. Roger screamed and his eardrums started to bleed. Suddenly, Roger was face to face Vyle.

"Pl... please..." Roger tried to plead.

Vyle reached out and viciously grabbed the back of Roger's head. He yanked him up into the air, breaking the chains. Roger's screams rang through the dungeon as his body dangled high above the ground like a rag doll.

"What... are you?" Roger cried.

Roger trembled as Vyle opened his mouth to once more feed on him. Roger helplessly watched as his ghostly reflection was being sucked into Vyle's silver mouth. And then, just as carelessly as he was yanked up into the air, Roger was thrown back to the ground. His body writhed in pain and he could no longer move.

A small purple light radiated from Vyle's fingertip. Roger felt Vyle tear off his shirt and then place a wet, rotting finger under his skin and on the bone of his spine. Alexia, hiding silently in the dark, watched the purple light start to trace through Roger's spinal cord. She could see Vyle shielding his face as the purple light began to flow through his veins. Vyle hissed as the light grew brighter and then burst into thick black smoke and ash. The smoke immediately wrapped around Roger and smothered the light.

Suddenly, Alexia felt her body slam against the wall. The monstrous King of the Nightmares stuck his skeletal face up against Alexia's and was now staring into her eyes. Alexia felt her neck burn as he gripped his silver claws around her neck and squeezed on her throat.

"I haven't forgotten about you," he hissed angrily and then slammed Alexia onto the ground.

Vyle gnashed his teeth and then disappeared into the darkness, slamming the metal door shut as he left. One by one the torches slowly lit the walls again. Alexia picked herself up and crawled over to Roger.

"Roger?" she whispered, reaching out to him.

Roger felt different. His legs did not hurt anymore, but his body was sore and he felt drained of energy. It took everything he had to sit up. He pushed his body against the cold wall, turned to Alexia, and asked,

"Wha... what happened?"

"That thing... it feeds on children, on us," she whispered.

"You look so... old."

"That's what happens to us when it feeds. Look," Alexia replied, pointing at a puddle of water close to Roger.

Roger wearily turned his head and saw his reflection. His hair was gray and he had aged tremendously. Every movement drained him. Roger fell back against the wall, his head spinning and eyelids growing heavy. He could barely stay conscious.

"I feel like I'm gonna pass out..." Roger whispered, then toppled over and fell face first onto the ground.

Alexia moved back into the darkness and curled up against the wall. She crossed her arms over her bloodied knees, buried her head, and quietly cried,

"Daddy..."

Chapter Nine: To Reflection City…

Birds sang softly and a breeze gently blew over Landon's face. The sun glowed and warmed his skin. Flowing water trickled nearby. Landon could feel tiny feet hopping around on his chest. He opened his eyes to discover a small brilliantly colored bird chirping and beaming up at him. The tiny bird hopped a little closer, tilted its head, and then shot up into the air. As it ascended into the dawning of a pastel sky it grew incredibly large. Landon marveled at the bird as it sprouted a second pair of colorful feathered wings and flew gracefully through the sky.

Landon sat up and rubbed the sleep out from his eyes and found himself in a beautifully charming garden. Flowing next to him was a river crystal blue stream. It looked as though millions of tiny stars were surfing upon the rippling water. Cherry blossom trees and graceful willow trees swayed in a calm wind while tiny white fluffy seeds floated through the garden.

Landon turned to find Jake and Jeckles snuggled up to each other on a soft green mound of grass under one of the cherry blossom trees. He smiled, and then quietly wandered over to the water. He knelt down, cupped his hands, and then placed them under the water's surface. Landon splashed the blue water on his face. It was cool and refreshing. Once more, he reached his hands back down and allowed the water to pool into his hands again.

When Landon pulled his hands up from of the water it did not drip or seep between his fingers. Instead, the cool water stayed within his hands, sparkling in the sunlight. Landon looked closer and saw that the sparkling actually came from tiny glittering fairies that were dancing upon the water. They smiled up at Landon and waved to him as he placed the water gently back into the river.

"Good morning Landon," said Simon, startling him with his unsettling voice.

"Oh. Simon. Uh… good morning," Landon said, quickly turning to see Simon sitting under a swaying willow tree behind him.

"Where are we?" Landon asked.

"You tell me."

"Is this a dream?" Landon questioned.

"It was. I watched this all appear just before dawn," pointing all around him at the garden, Simon looked up at the beautiful sky, admiring the same bird Landon had been watching and then responded.

"Did we pretend?"

"It seems so," said Simon.

Landon suddenly remembered the pain that followed and waited for it. The pain never came. Strange as it was, Landon did not complain and even though it may not have been him pretending. He looked around and saw the round door they entered sitting freely on top of a small green mound of grass.

"We are still in the room. How is this possible, Simon?"

"In the land of Nod, imagination rules and has no reason or law. You and all the other imaginations before you made everything here. I have seen nothing like this, but it doesn't surprise me," said Simon as he wandered around, admiring the beautiful garden.

Simon walked over to Jeckles and lightly tapped him on his forehead. Jeckles drooled a little and rolled over before opening his eyes. Suddenly, he burst high into the air and screamed,

"Gagh! Where are we?"

Jake awoke to Jeckles screaming and sat straight up with wide eyes. He too was caught off guard by the garden and jumped up into a fighting stance. Simon grabbed Jeckles from hovering in the air and set him down on the soft green grass.

"We are still in the room. Everything is okay. Somehow you or Landon, maybe even Jeckles or all three of you created this while you slept. I have never seen this before but it does explain why Sentinel believes you to be dangerous. Although, I see nothing dangerous here… except for those, maybe," said Simon, pointing a long finger at a mound of various snacks and goodies, their wrappers glittering in the sun.

"Jake talks in his sleep… about food."

"I was definitely dreaming about food, I'm starving," said Jake delightfully.

The boys ran to the large mound of snacks, grabbed a few cereal bars, and a couple of neon orange bottles labeled 'Fruggle Juice'.

"What is Fruggle juice?" Landon asked.

"Fruggle juice is my favorite!" shouted excitedly.

"Sour Nedstiddle Norks? Gert's Gooey Gum Bots? Bearded Barry's Bigglestraws?" said Jake, reading off the labels while they dug through the heaping mound of food.

"Check this out, fellas. Oggy Boogy Tarts, Ever Glazed Sugar Cookie Donuts, and Mrs. Neat's No Mess Muffins! These are foods we have here in Nod," shouted Jeckles, shoving them into his mouth, some still in their wrappers, and eating them.

"The first sun is up. Jeckles, we must take them to Madam Roma."

Simon pulled Jeckles out from the mound of food and then led the way back to the door. One by one, they exited the serene garden and found themselves in the hallway of Simon's home. Only this time, besides the door they just left, there was only one other door sitting at the end of the now short hallway. The rest were gone and upon shutting the door behind them, it too vanished. Landon was still trying to understand why he had no pain and quietly asked Jake,

"Did your head hurt at all this morning?"

"No," said Jake.

"Neither did mine."

"You okay, man?" Jake asked giving Landon a friendly shove into the hallway.

"Yeah, I'm good. Just trying to wrap my head around all this."

Jake shoved a cereal bar into his mouth and shrugged his shoulders as they walked towards an incredibly tall wooden door with a skull shaped window. Twisted bits of wrought iron reached across the door and spiraled into the glass mouth of the skull. Bone white skeletons gracefully danced in a row across the smooth iron surface. As they disappeared into the window the glass rippled in different colors and like the reflection of light in water.

"Simon, is that the front door?" Landon asked.

"Yes, and my favorite. Allow me."

Simon placed a finger on top of the bronze door knob that looked like a closed eyeball and then traced his sharp fingernail around it. As he did, a beautiful golden circle sparkled along the surface of the knob and the eye slowly opened, sleepily looking around until it saw Simon. And then, the door opened.

"After you," said Simon, welcoming them out the door.

Landon stepped out onto a wide and rickety wooden porch. It was crooked, badly weathered, and balanced on a narrow ledge, swaying in the wind. Up in the pastel pink and purple sky, the birds from the garden were now flying by, heading towards Reflection City. There were two suns, one orange and brightly rising while the other was barely peeking, casting a soft purple hue across the horizon. The clouds were the fluffiest clouds Landon had ever seen and, even with both Suns rising, he could still see the stars twinkling just as bright as if it were night. Simon shut the door behind him and stepped off the porch then leaned over the ledge, scanning the ground below.

"Does it always look like this?" Landon asked.

"Yes. Always," Simon answered

"Gagh! Get off my foot you freakin' slimy, little, bowling bowl sized booger!" Jake shouted as Jeckles rolled right over his foot.

Jeckles popped up into the air, instantly turned a bright red, and angrily replied,

"I am not a booger and you, mate, are rude!"

He then crossed his candy cane arms and grumbled to Simon,

"Do we have to take him with us?"

"What? I didn't ask to be here. You guys brought me here against my will, albeit to save us from Vyle. But then, you locked me in a closet! Which, by the way, was completely dark and smelled like old socks!"

"Now, you roll over my foot, get mad at me, and have the audacity to ask if you have to take me with? Oh, you're taking me with you, you little goblin! And, you're going to get me back home safe and sound like I was before I met you!"

"I'm not slimy! I am clean and smooth!" shouted Jeckles, whipping out his cane and whacking Jake in his shin.

Jake felt the snap of his cane and immediately chased after him. Jeckles quickly rolled up onto Simon's shoulder, where he knew Jake could not reach him, and pointed the bottom of his cane into Jake's forehead, yelling,

"Rude, rude, rude. Rude!"

Jake fell back and flipped Jeckles his middle finger. Jeckles mimicked the gesture causing Landon and Simon to burst into laughter. Jake's anger faded and he began to laugh as well. As he rubbed the sting out of his shin, he looked up at Jeckles and asked,

"Well, how do we get down from here, chuckles?"

"First, tell me I'm not slimy!"

"Fine. You're not slimy," Jake huffed.

"Tell me I'm pretty." Jeckles teased.

"You're pretty,"

"Aw, thank y… "

"You're pretty slimy!" Jake interrupted, causing Landon and Simon to burst into another round of laughter.

After the laughter died, Simon pointed towards the edge of the cliff and without a single hint of sarcasm, said,

"Jump."

Both Landon and Jake took a few steps backward with large and solemn eyes.

"You're kidding, right?" Landon asked.

Jeckles rolled down off of Simon to the edge of the cliff and, with what sounded like a tiny fart, he jumped off the edge. The boys ran and cautiously peered over to see where he went. Jeckles was falling quickly. As he descended, he rolled over and once more, flipped his middle finger and then vanished below a sea of marshmallow clouds.

"Did he really just fart and then give us the finger?" asked Jake surprisingly.

"Yep."

Suddenly, a dark shadow quickly passed over their heads. Simon dove over them head first and disappeared into the thick clouds.

"No. Not happening. Nope. No. No! There is no way I am jumping off this cliff," said Jake firmly, searching for another way down.

Landon shared Jake's sentiment and went with him. As they made their way back to the house, Landon could see the swaying residence in its entirety. It was a crooked stone tower with a shingled cone roof pointing sharply into the sky. The base of the tower and the wooden porch were much larger than the thin ledge it sat upon, leaving no way around the house without falling off the cliff.

"This is just ridiculous! Landon! Can't you imagine some, like, safe stairway down to the ground?"

"That's not a bad idea," Landon answered.

Landon walked back to the edge and knelt down. He closed his eyes and pictured a stairway with iron rails, leading down from the nose of the cliff's ledge. Nothing happened. Both he and Jake took turns, managing only to get a few shaking planks that hovered for a moment before plummeting below. Then, after deciding to give it one last shot, stairs began to appear and stay.

"It's working! I can see the stairs folding down into the clouds," screamed Jake.

Pain sliced into Landon's head and broke his concentration. He fell back and waited for the pain to pass. When it did, he looked over the edge to see what he created. There, hovering below one another, without touching at all, were a spiral of glass steps. There were no handrails, and the steps swayed a little in the wind.

"Seriously?" Landon asked rhetorically.

"After you then," said Jake, lightly nudging Landon forward.

Landon laid flat on his belly, reaching his hand out to the first step, and then pushed down on it. The step gave a little and then resisted his efforts. Once he let go, the glass plank returned to its original place. Landon stood up and placed his foot on the step. Again, the step gave a little. He waited and after a moment, it balanced him.

Taking in a deep breath, Landon brought his other foot down onto the step. It did not budge at all. Full of relief, he sighed and began to slowly make his way down. After getting down a few steps, Landon turned around to see how Jake was doing. He was standing with one foot on the cliff and the other on the first step.

Jake stepped down, found his balance, and let out a sigh of relief, quickly following Landon. After successfully climbing down several steps, Jake stopped and looked out at the beautiful fluffy ocean of colorful clouds, rolling below. Suddenly, the glass under his foot cracked. Jake looked up and saw the glass steps above starting to crack as well.

"They're going to break!" Jake screamed.

Landon looked back and saw the steps above cracking. Both he and Jake rushed down each step, trying to be as fast and careful as possible. Landon hurriedly jumped down onto step and found himself standing above the thick rolling clouds. He could not see the next step and Jake was already behind him ready to jump. Suddenly, the step beneath Landon's feet cracked. He took in a deep breath and then jumped.

The cloud was thick and Landon could feel himself passing through it, he was falling. Within the clouds were flashes of neon lights strobing to what sounded like a Pink Floyd song. As Landon gained more speed, it looked as though he were falling through a laser light show.

Landon broke free from the clouds and saw that he was plummeting dangerously fast towards the desert below. Suddenly, Jake fell through the clouds, screaming,

"This is so not cool!"

The ground was nearing, and both of the boys braced for impact. Landon closed his eyes and waited for the end. The rushing air became quiet and his clothes became still. There was a moment of complete silence and stillness. Landon opened his eyes and discovered himself and Jake suspended a few feet above the sand. They slowly floated down onto the sweeping sands. Jake immediately dropped to his hands and knees, kissing the ground and spitting out little granules of sand as he repeatedly whispered,

"Oh, thank you! Thank you! Thank you!"

"It's about time. What took you so long?" interrupted Jeckles, who was sitting with Simon on a large rock, waiting for them to come down.

"Nice stairs. Should have jumped though. The drop's way better from the top."

Simon agreed and then motioned for everyone to follow him into the rolling desert.

"The path is hidden, but not from me. Make sure you follow me closely and walk only where I walk. If you don't, you could get swept out into the desert by one of those rolling dunes," Simon instructed, pointing out into the ocean waves of sand.

"This is amazing, Simon," said Landon as Simon began to walk, motioning for them to follow

"You haven't seen anything yet!"

The hours of the day quickly passed as they trekked through the desert and the first sun was starting to set behind dunes with the second quickly following. The path must have become difficult for Simon to keep track of. A few times, they had to stop, and wait for Simon to find it. While they waited, Jeckles gave them all water. Once again, seemingly pulling it out of nowhere.

"We are close. Just over that hill," said Simon, pointing to a dune that was not moving ahead of them.

Simon moved forward and easily climbed up to the top of the dune. Landon and Jake followed, climbing as fast as they could, fighting to keep solid footing. Jeckles curled up into a ball and began to spin in place, building up speed. As he rocketed up the sand dune and past the boys, a stream of sand sprayed them.

When they reached the top Jake shot Jeckles a mean stare as he brushed the sand off of him. Jeckles had a sorrowful expression on his face and only looked at Jake from the side of his eyes.

Landon looked up and saw a silver gate. It was glowing brightly and sat free from any structure, slightly hunched over. To Landon it looked like it was sleeping, just like the refrigerator in Simon's kitchen. Floating above the gate was an arched banner that shimmered like diamonds and read, 'Welcome'.

"We have reached the city gates. I cannot go in this way, but I will meet you in the tunnels," said Simon.

"So, from here on in, you two, stick with me," Jeckles chimed in happily.

"What? Why?" asked Jake.

"Because they outcast him. How do you get in?" Landon answered.

"The shadowsyde."

"The shadow side?" Jake questioned.

"It used to be a passageway from place to place here in Nod. Dreamers would slip into this passageway and be transported to wherever they desired to go. Nightmares found the entrance in Del Toro. Vyle and his horde of Nightmares transformed the shadowsyde into their own dark highway. Because of Del Toro, almost all the entrances have been sealed to protect Nod."

Landon looked out past the gate and could see the bright city far off in the distance. In fact, it was so far away it looked just as far as it did when he first saw it from Simon's room.

"How is it that the city is still so far away?" Landon asked, pointing his finger at the shimmering city.

"Yeah, what's that all about? That's like a billion miles from here, man," said Jake shaking his head in disbelief.

"Ever since the Nightmare attacks, to get into Reflection City you have to use special gates. They were made by the Sandmen to protect the cities and traveling Dreamers. The gate will take you right into the city," Simon answered.

Jeckles turned to the gate, took in a deep breath, and then dragged his hand across the glowing poles of the hunched over gate. Like a harp, it played a sweet melody and made the gate stand straight up and open its doors. A cool, sweet smelling air surrounded them and carried a nostalgic aroma into Landon's nose. The smell reminded him of being a newborn. As the gates fully opened, a brilliant white light beamed through the entry and practically blinded Jake and Landon. Jeckles whipped out a large pair of sunglasses, gave finger guns to the boys, and then disappeared into the blinding light, shouting,

"See you on the other side."

Landon took in a deep breath and crossed the threshold. Neon colors raced through his vision and made him dizzy. When his vision cleared, he saw Jeckles and Jake standing next to him, rubbing their eyes clear. In front of the gate stood a small wooden platform with a giant light bulb pointed towards the entrance. A Dreamer that looked like a raccoon jumped down from the platform and ran up to Jeckles. They exchanged a few hushed words and a few candy bars were exchanged before the Dreamer turned to the boys and introduced himself.

"Hi, name's Teddy. Never met a real kid before. Welcome to Reflection City."

"Wrap these around your heads and follow me, quickly," Jeckles instructed, tossing over a couple long scarves to the boys and then rolling into the foliage of a nearby garden where he settled into a gathering of bushes.

"Well, you heard him," said Teddy while munching on a candy bar.

They both wrapped their heads and hid their faces, then ran over to Jeckles. Once they were in the garden, Landon peeked through the bushes to see. The garden sat on a hill that overlooked the glittering city. Shimmering gloriously over Reflection City, Landon could see the Fountain of Dreams and its beautiful waterfall pouring down from the sky. The city was enormous and littered in strings of colorful lights glowing so brightly that there was a hardly any shadows within the city.

Buildings were walking, shuffling through the streets like giant people without arms. Strange vehicles roamed the streets and flew through the sky. Out in the distance, some of the buildings were playing tag, causing bits of their walls to crumble and fall, almost crushing passing Dreamers below. Others simply sat still and swayed in a gentle breeze that carried a sweet aroma of freshly baked pumpkin pie. To Landon, the city felt alive and he was in complete awe of it.

"Stay down!" Jeckles snapped, pulling Landon, who had unknowingly stood up, back down into the bushes.

A loud roar came from above and a rushing wind blew through the garden, threatening to reveal their location. The boys remained motionless as they watched a flying bus with several white feathered wings and a dangerously sharp bee stinger on its end dive over them and towards the road in front of the garden. It halted on its nose before crashing into the ground and then slammed its body down onto the red pavement of the road. Next, the bus smoothly pulled up to a stop sign where a large group of Dreamers were waiting.

"We must hurry before anyone sees you. We will go through that alley. Stay out of the shadows! Ready? Let's go!" Jeckles whispered, pointing them towards a tiny alley down the street and then speedily rolling away towards it.

The boys raced out of the garden and down onto the street, following Jeckles to the alley. As they broke free from the bushes and ran down the hill, Landon fell and rolled out onto the street. A large blue Dreamer wearing pink overalls and a yellow hard hat leaned out the bus door, looked over at Landon, and shouted,

"Hey buddy! You okay? Want me to hold the door?"

Landon shook his head and the big blue Dreamer disappeared into the bus. He picked himself up and then ran to the alley. Jeckles was standing under a string of lights, tapping his foot impatiently. He shot both boys a dirty look and then said in a serious tone,

"Stay in the light and don't stop running. Go!"

Jeckles and the boys took off down the long dimly lit alley, trying to stay within safety of the lights that hung above their heads. In the gaps, Landon could see the darkness swimming with movement. As they raced through the alley, Landon thought he saw flashes of purple fire within a few of the dark spots. They quickly neared the end of the alley and Landon noticed there were no more lights, just darkness. Suddenly, Jeckles disappeared and Jake screamed,

"I don't wanna die!"

Chapter Ten: A Nightmare Rises...

Nestled within a murderous mountain range, near the coast of a freezing ocean that pounds its poisonous waves upon blackened shores, is the tortured city of Vey. Vyle's putrid kingdom in the nightmarish underbelly of Nyx. A place that reeks of death.

Sounds of teeth chattering, chains clanking, and wind whistling echoed off the ruins of a decayed city, singing an eerie lullaby through the night. Darkness smothers the streets and its lurking residents like a wet blanket, suffocating everything as the wind howled through leafless trees and broken windows of crooked and haunting structures.

A tower of smoke, spiraling up into the starless sky like an upside-down tornado perched upon the tip of a steep mountain top, stood high above the bent and torturous landscape below. Flowing in the opposite direction around the base of the whirling tower was a thick blood-red moat with a rusted metal bridge that lead to a set of enormous doors that stood unaffected by the spinning walls.

Deep within the twisting tower, a sharp and painful throne made from jagged shards of metal and screaming faces, twisting in pain, sat high above a rolling sea of wretched Nightmares. Starring menacingly from upon high the deathly throne, shrouded in black leather and rusted metal armor, sat Lord Vyle, digging his long silver claws into the eyes of two screaming faces. His emerald eyes flickering as he looked down at his dark court, gnashing their silver teeth and waiting for the king to speak. A crown of long blackened blades ripped through his tightly wrapped pale skin, stretching high up over his skeletal head as long ropes of chain clinked at the side of his throne like a pack of dogs, awaiting their master's command. And, after a few moments, his eyes flashed brightly, suddenly bringing the roaring ocean of evil complete silence.

"The time is nearing!" Vyle shouted, his voice booming like a lion's roar through the tower and erupting the Nightmares below into a fierce cheer.

From behind his throne, a thin and putrid Nightmare named Shreak, inched closer to Vyle. As he did, he lowered his eyes, crookedly leaned over and bowed to his king, asking with a voice that sounded like nails on a chalk board.

"What is your command, my master?"

Vyle's eyes flamed wildly, causing Shreak to shudder and cower. Then, turned his gaze back down onto the ocean of Nightmares below his throne. Vyle stood up from his cruel throne and raised his arms over the crowd.

"I am your king, your master, your lord! Their world is destined for darkness! And, I will deliver it! Soon, we attack again." Vyle roared, sending the wretched crowd into horrible frenzy of praise and cheer.

Vyle returned to his throne, crossed his long claws over his silver teeth while he starred out over the sea of joyous Nightmares, and then said to Shreak,

"Raise the Reapers from their sleep. Bring me Bones."

Shreak nodded, bowed, and then flew down from the throne and disappeared into the ocean of smoke and darkness below. The Nightmares hissed and screamed with horrid delight, quickly following Shreak out of the tower. Bursting through the iron doors, they flew down through the decayed city to an enormous pit at its center. A pit so incredibly dark, it swallows light.

The Nightmares circled the pit and raised their rotting fists high into the air, chanting loudly. Shreak perched himself upon its edge and stared into the black abyss. He retrieved a small gray pouch from within his tattered robe, unraveled the white cord keeping it closed, and poured red ash from within it into the pit.

"From the Veil, we summon you. From Death's realm, the chosen few. A Reapers oath to the sprouting seeds. When the harvest comes, you will be reaped," Shreak chanted along with the circling Nightmares.

The ground began to shake and the eyes of the surrounding Nightmares burned wildly as a thick stream of blood shot up out of the pit like a geyser. Six skeletal Reapers with silver skulls hovered high above the pit, emptily starring down upon the chanting Nightmares with hollow eye sockets. Their skeletal bodies were covered in bits of black armor, long chains dangling from the bones of their exposed rib cages. Each Reaper with four massive wings of oily smoke stretching out a few dozen feet behind them; their bodies riddled with black flames that licked wildly at the air. In their right armored hand, a long scythe with a blade as red blood and snath made of bone. Shreak raised his rotten fist above his head and silenced his fellow Nightmares.

"Bones," he screeched to the Reapers.

The Reapers did not speak. They simply raised their scythes above their heads and flew away into the freezing night, their wings staining the sky behind them. As Shreak and the rest of the Nightmares in Vey watched, Vyle remained seated upon his throne, deep in thought. With a wave of his silver clawed hand, several ropes of rusted chain shot out from behind his throne and into the darkness in front of him. They raced through the tower, clanging through long corridors, cutting around stone corners, and twisting down dangerous stair cases until they burst through a small metal hatch, into a pitch-black hole where they wrapped tightly around a thin and ragged man, choking him and wrenching him from his slumber.

The chains yanked the frail man through the tower without any regard for his body as he smashed into walls and flew across the floor. In mere seconds, he was slammed down in front of the terrifying throne and king of Nightmares. Vyle stood up and slowly approached the battered man. Barely able to breathe and unable to move, the frail man began to tremble. Vyle gnashed his teeth together at the sight, his eyes flickering. Vyle knelt down and placed one sharp claw under the man's chin, cutting into the flesh while raising his head up. Vyle pointed at the smooth black floor in the center of his massive throne room and grinned as a hole opened up.

A dark Endindrium, encased in an oval frame of black smoke and dripping oil, floated up from the opening. Green and black fire hypnotically spiraled within its rippling purple surface as it hovered. Vyle let loose of the man's chin and shoved his head down into the floor, standing up and then making his way to the Endindrium.

"Is it not beautiful, Sandman?" Vyle asked, tracing his silver claws over the frame and then across the mirror's surface.

"Allow me to thank you for making it."

Vyle lifted his clawed fist and commanded the chains to twist tightly around the feeble Sandman's body, cutting into his body from head to toe. Blood streamed out from the chains cutting into his forehead and filled his mouth. The thick liquid poured down his throat and started to spill into his lungs, causing him to choke. The smell of flesh cooking filled the throne room as the chains began to glow hot and sear the man's skin.

Through it all, the Sandman did not scream. He stayed silent. His eyes however, smiled through the torture. Deep within the labyrinth of his mind, like a star caught in the night of his pupils, twinkled a secret. Vyle forced the Sandman to create his own Endindrium, one specially made for a Nightmare. A dark Endindrium that he uses to steal children. Slowly, with every use, an invisible fracture grows within the Endindrium. When it finally

shatters, it will take whoever that unfortunate being is to a sadistic

place where Nightmares are cute-cuddly teddy bears compared to

the demons imprisoned there. An infernal hell known as Euval.

Chapter Eleven: The Underground...

As Landon and Jake faded into the darkness at the end of

the alley, they quickly discovered that it had transformed into

Large tunnel with rows upon rows of colorful string lights.

Suddenly, Simon's frightening voice whispered from behind them,

"Welcome to the Underground."

"For crying out loud!" Jake shouted, both boys startled by

Simon's sudden arrival.

Landon and Jake took a moment to catch their breath and

calm their nerves before following Simon and Jeckles into

the Underground. As they navigated through the dazzling tunnels,

Jeckles rolled next to them, weaving in and out of Simon's giant

steps.

"It was you back there wasn't it? Standing in the dark?"

Landon asked Simon.

"Yes."

"Was it you making all those purple flashes in the dark parts of the alley too, like the fire in your house?" Jake questioned.

"Yes," Simon answered, igniting a small purple fireball in his palm. "Because I am part Nightmare, I can travel undetected by Dreamers in the shadows, but I still have to be careful."

"I am not sure if a Nightmare can still finish the job that Vyle started and completely change me. Ever since the night, I can feel this fire burning inside me, all the way down into my bones. It doesn't hurt anymore."

"One night while I was traveling the shadowsyde to Reflection City, I was followed by a Nightmare. I was terrified it was going to catch me. The more anxious I became, the more I felt this fire within me building and building. Suddenly, these purple flames burst from both of my hands and whatever was following me disappeared."

Landon and Jake watched as Simon made the fire dance from fingertip to fingertip.

"Man, that is awesome!" exclaimed Jake with a wide grin plastered across his face.

"I believe that some of the power Vyle gained from you when he fed, was also poured into me as I was changing. Once I discovered this ability, I have used this fire to protect myself from the Nightmares hiding in the shadows. They hate it."

"How did you learn that you could travel in the shadows?" Landon asked.

Simon traced his finger upon a cord of Christmas lights as they walked through the hall.

"Before that Night, before the city had all these lights up, there were no gates or hidden entrances. There was no need for protection because Nod had never seen a Nightmare. Del Toro was first, after, Vyle and his wretched hordes attacked city after city. Torturing Dreamers and gaining knowledge until he decided to change them into Nightmares. That is how Vyle learned about Nod and her secrets."

"With the help of Deity, Sentinel and the Sandmen have enchanted many city gates and entrances. Dreamers have found ways of brightening where they live and do their best to fight off the growing shadows and dark spots swarming with Nightmares, lurking within their city."

Landon could tell, even through the eeriness of Simon's voice, that he felt solely responsible for everything that has occurred. As they wandered silently through the glowing tunnels under the moving city, Jeckles grew tired and rolled up onto Jake's shoulders, straddling the back of his neck and holding onto the top of his head like a child.

"Get off me!" Jake screamed as he attempted to pull Jeckles off.

"I'm so tired, mate. Just carry me!" Jeckles whined as he struggled to hold onto Jake's head by grabbing his hair.

Simon and Landon shared in a laugh as they watched Jake spin around, trying to shake Jeckles off. Eventually, he did and then drop kicked Jeckles like a football down the tunnel.

Landon was laughing so hard that it made Jake start to chuckle. Jeckles on the other hand was not happy. In fact, he quickly rolled back, right over both of Jakes feet before popping up next to Simon and flipping both of his middle fingers up at Jake.

"So, what is this 'Underground'?" Landon asked.

"So glad you asked," Jeckles answered, pleased by Landon's curiosity.

"Before Simon was the oh-so beautiful and handsome guy he is today, I was assigned to be his mentor and prepare him with the best knowledge that any Dreamer could ask for. After all, I am the smartest Dreamer you'll ever meet. But, I digress. The day Simon was banished, Sentinel brought him before all of the Dreamers in Reflection City. They labeled him a 'Frightener' and then cast him out. Forbidding him to ever return."

Simon's shoulders dropped a little and Landon heard him sigh under his bandaged face. It was obvious, ever since that night, guilt weighed heavily on him.

"Quick sidenote, there's a group of us who have and will always consider Simon family. And, even though it's been declared forbidden, nothing will stop us from seeing him... ever!" said Jeckles shooting a quick wink up at Simon.

"Anyway, on the night of the first attack here on Reflection City, I was chased by a handful... no, a league, of Nightmares!"

Simon shook his head and held up one finger at the boys. Silently correcting Jeckles and informing them that he had been chased by a single Nightmare. Jeckles shrugged his shoulders, his eyes growing three times bigger as he stared down the tunnel, and continued,

"Fine, one Nightmare... but, it was humongous! Biggest Nightmare you ever saw. It chased me into that alley back there and as I ran, I kept thinking this is it, it's all over for me. That's when it happened. I felt myself falling through the darkness. It felt like an eternity, but once I hit the bottom I found myself laying on top of our good friend Dozer."

"Dozer is a Sandman, nicest one around. Anyway, he had a long shining stick that had this bright light on the end of it and when the Nightmare came in after me, he burned it to a crisp! Together, we found this place buried under the city. We explored the tunnels, trying to find a way out and when we did, the city was in pretty bad shape."

"I returned to the group with Dozer and we all came back down here to make sure no one else had fallen in here and clear out any Nightmares that might have been hiding under our city. We patrolled the tunnels for weeks, putting up all these lights, making it safe. And, with Dozer's help, this place has a special enchantment that keeps us magically hidden from Sentinel. He was the one who so wonderfully named these tunnels and this sanctuary, the Underground," Jeckles concluded with an air of victory.

"I don't get it. Why is the alley still hidden in the dark?" Landon asked curiously.

"Another wonderful question! We keep the entrance to the Underground in the dark for two reasons. First, to give Simon a way to enter the city without being seen. Which simultaneously

keeps unwanted Dreamers out and discovering our secret.

Second, even though the shadows can be accessed by Nightmares,

Simon can lead them into the entrance where they have, on

many occasions, gone up in smoke. As

you noticed upon entering the Underground, it's fairly bright down

here and with Dozer's enchantment on the entry, there is

no way out except through exit which just happens to be way on

the other side, and is also illuminated by a few million lights,"

Jeckles continued as he pointed at the lights surrounding them.

"So, no Nightmare can enter. Otherwise..." Jake

questioned.

"Otherwise..." Jeckles whispered, sliding a finger across

what would be his neck and then making gurgling sounds as he

dramatically fell to the floor.

"We are here," Simon interjected, ushering the boys around

the corner to a magnificent golden door.

Jeckles immediately sped over to the golden door, popped up, and then knocked rapidly with momentary pauses between every few knocks. The door opened, and they entered into a concrete room with a dome ceiling covered in, what could have easily been, hundreds of thousands of beautiful twinkling lights. In the center of the room were several Dreamers sitting at a round and weathered table.

"Now, I warn you, our friends might be a tad curious when they meet you both," Jeckles whispered as the group of Dreamers excitedly approached.

"Are they... real children?" asked a small Dreamer swimming in an oversized orange sweater that hid his mouth and covered his entire body except for the tips of his brown shoes.

"Yes," Simon answered.

"This is Jake and this is Landon," said Simon as they stepped forward.

"Hi. What's your name?" Landon asked, shaking the little Dreamer's hand.

"My name is, Sweet Tooth!" said the wide-eyed little Dreamer.

"Allow me to introduce you to, Madam Roma," said Simon with great admiration.

"She can pretend," Jeckles whispered through the side of his mouth.

Madam Roma stepped forward and bowed. She wore a red flowing dress with many small golden bells that dangled from thin gold chains and was very elegant in her movements. She wore a sheer pink scarf wrapped around her neck and over her long black hair, like a hood.

"Good evening," she said softly.

A large black cat with a saddle and a large cannon strapped to it, stepped forward and slightly bowed his head to the boys. He wore a black collar that had a large silver bone hanging from it with his name engraved on it. Mad Jack ensured the boys saw it by placing it directly in their faces while purring loudly next to Simon, who was petting him.

"This is, Mad Jack," Simon continued.

"And, me am Frank," said a large block-like Dreamer, stepping forward.

"Yes, you are. Frank, meet Landon and Jake," Simon replied.

Frank reached out his large hand and, to the boys' surprise, shook their hands rather gently. He wore a white button up shirt that stretched tightly across his block frame, a burgundy blazer in which the sleeves were too short, showing his two thick wrists that were wrapped in metal cuffs with broken chains dangling from them. Frank also wore a pair of black pants tucked into some dirty unlaced gray leather boots. He had limp black hair that seemed to grow only on the top of his head, hanging over his protruding brow and eyes like a curtain, and a large under bite in which his lower teeth sat sticking out of his mouth, sort of like a bulldog.

"And, finally…" Simon whispered playfully as he pointed to two small rag doll Dreamers that bounced all around them.

"These two Halloweenies are, Lynn, and Anne."

"Ahem," said one of the little rag dolls.

Jeckles raised an eyebrow curiously and then snapped his fingers and pointed at a small pink heart shaped pocket on Anne's tiny Halloweenie chest.

"Actually, there's one more."

"Ah yes, how could I have forgotten?" said Simon.

"The wild, the brave, the most cosmically magical in all the land, Anastasia." said Jeckles as he bowed to a very tiny rag doll tucked safely within Anne's heart shaped pocket.

"I'm Anne," said the little Halloweenie, who was jumping high into the air with her light curly brown ribbon hair flopping up and down as she held onto the itty-bitty smiling Anastasia in her pocket.

Anne wore a purple and pink dress with pink thread sewn into her large brown button eyes and danced around a giant Halloween pumpkin trick or treat basket she had set down next to her.

"And, I'm Lynn," said the other Halloweenie.

Lynn had dark black ribbon hair tied in pig tails with green lace and small sugar skulls, and giant black button eyes with green thread sewn threw them. She wore a green dress with bits of red upon her chest and had another sugar skull hanging from her green pearl necklace.

"We're the Halloweenies!" they said together and then ran over to Jeckles and crawled all over him making him laugh.

"So, this is the group. Group, this is my creator, Landon, and his friend, Ja..." Simon tried to say, but was interrupted by a loud erupting sound that echoed through the room in which Lynn turned to Anne and yelled,

"Ew! You farted!"

Anne shook her head and pinched the areas where both her and little Anastasia's noses should have been and replied nasally,

"No way. That was you!"

They looked at each other, then looked at Jeckles and saw him suspiciously rolling his eyes and whistling.

"It was you!" they screamed simultaneously and then ran away from Jeckles, who immediately chased after them.

The rest of the Dreamers laughed and followed Simon as he motioned to sit at the table. After everyone sat down and Jeckles convinced the others he was done expelling gas, Madam Roma spoke,

"Let's call this meeting to order."

She made a small green mallet appear out of a green smoke that came from her hand and she smacked it down on the table. In the center of the table, a crystal ball appeared and hovered above a deep blue velvet table cloth that suddenly draped over the table.

"You can pretend!" said Jake to Madam Roma who smiled and nodded.

"Nice! Does your head hurt after?"

"Not anymore."

"Why does it hurt?" he asked.

"Like any muscle, to align your imagination clearly with your ability to manifest, you have to train that part of your mind.

Like learning to crawl and then stand. With practice, the pain will fade."

Simon leaned in and placed his long hands on the table, cleared his throat which silenced everyone, then spoke to Madam Roma directly,

"It was just as you said. Vyle found a way back. That means..." Simon paused.

"Yes," Madam Roma sighed, shook her head, and then closed her eyes.

"He has Dozer."

Madam Roma opened her eyes, stared deeply into the hovering crystal ball, and began mumbling quietly under her breath. The crystal ball started to spin and fill with black smoke, embers, and ash. Landon became hypnotized, staring into the dark smoke and glittering red embers swirling inside, and felt his mind drifting.

The smoke slowly dissipated and when it cleared, Landon could see a chubby purple bird with tiny wings standing in the middle of a glittering dirt road, twitching and hopping around in circles.

Once more, the smoke kicked up and began spinning within the crystal ball. Embers and ash swirled violently, shaking the ball. Madam Roma's eyes widened as the crystal cracked and the smoke poured out and spilled down over them, quickly flooding the room. A huge gust of wind suddenly swirled around the table and spun the smoke around them like they were caught in the eye of a tornado, desperately holding onto the table to keep from being sucked up into the spiraling smoke.

"What's happening?" Landon yelled.

Suddenly, everything had become still and silent. Landon was no longer clinging to a table, nor was he seated. Landon was floating in an empty white space, alone. As he hovered, weightless, Landon saw a speck in the distance appear and then start to grow. It was moving towards him.

As the speck came close enough to see clearly, Landon could see it was a dark ring with a small clear stone and looked like it was made out of black bone. He reached out his hand and the ring gently rested onto the center of his palm. Landon stared into the diamond, it was like a window to deep space. Stars twinkled as comets shot across fantasy landscapes of colorful gas clouds. Floating within the cosmos of the stone was of a massive white tree, its leaves were dripping with blood. From above the tree, three golden circles of light appeared and then wrapped around it, making it glow. The tree began to beam, filling the stone and the space around Landon with a brilliantly blinding white light. Suddenly, he felt his body on the ground and heard Jake calling out to him,

"Landon! Hey, man!"

Landon shook off the confusion and opened his eyes to see Jake shaking and slapping him with the crowd of Dreamers staring over him.

"Wha… What happened?" Landon asked.

"You got hit by part of the crystal ball, man. It totally exploded and smashed into your head!" Jake replied as he helped Landon back up onto his feet.

"No, I saw something!"

"A vision. What did you see?" asked Madam Roma.

Landon stood up and felt his head rush with blood, making him dizzy and challenging his equilibrium. So much so, that Jake and Simon had to catch him before he fell back over. After a moment, his vision cleared, and slowly answered,

"I… um… there was a white room and there was this black ring. I held it in my hand. I saw space, some kind of bird, and this stone… it… it was so bright. There was this tree. The leaves… they were bleeding. What does it mean?"

"Death's Hand," whispered Madam Roma.

Chapter Twelve: The Knucklebone...

High in the clouds above Nod, thunder rolled deeply as lightning flashed like electric veins across the storming sky. Soaring within the raging storm was a steam punk pirate ship with giant cogs grinding and tubes pumping as loud as, if not louder than, the thunderous cracks exploding across the sky. The raging storm doused its rain like wet needles upon the stern face of a tall and broad-shouldered man standing behind the wheel of the flying ship and strong against the stinging rain and violent winds. Even as it began to hail rocks of ice at him, still he did not move. The fierce man rooted his feet to the deck and grinned.

Across the ship and through the howling winds, hundreds of Skybogs sang a sea shanty. They were little green and yellow goblins that operated the ship as it soared through the violent storm. Several steaming pipes screamed throughout the ship and cut through the storm and grinding gears clanged loudly from the engines as the Skybogs shifted the direction of the enormous flying ship.

Through the angry skies of Nod, pushing the steam powered metal engines so hard that sparks exploded over the grinding gears and rattled the wooden framing, they flew deeper into the storm. Several of the Skybogs had to quickly wrench the giant steel bolts that started to loosen from their iron braces back into their homes to keep the ship's frame from breaking.

Burgundy sails were released from their tightly rolled slumber and dropped from several beautifully engraved wooden and steel masts. Upon the tallest mast, that only the Captain could touch, flew his colors, a tattered burgundy flag with the image of black crossbones with a black skull over them. The lower mandible was missing and written down the center of skull and from under each eye socket were several white symbols. The flag waved boldly above the massive flying pirate ship as the fierce man stared daringly into the storm. He stood fearless and focused. His name, Bagsuv Bones - Captain of the Knucklebone, ruler of the Skybogs, and master of the skies of Nod!

Captain Bones stood tall above his crew in a black over coat with several burgundy belts and silver buckles laid over a charcoal vest cream button shirt. Tucked behind his overcoat was a sword sheathed in a jewel encrusted scabbard and flintlock pistol that he tapped the rings on his left hand upon while steering the Knucklebone through the storming sky with his other. His long silver hair and beard blowing wildly in the wind as the Knucklebone ascended higher into the temperamental clouds.

Lightning suddenly struck one of the masts and sent an electric pulse through a small Skybog that instantly popped straight up into the air and fell right back down on its face. After a minute, the tiny little charred Skybog shook off the high voltage shock, got back up, and resumed his duties. The faster they flew, the harder the wind fought to bring them down.

As the Knucklebone pierced through the clouds, high above the drowning land below, the ship's metal appendages expanded and contracted straining its wooden body. The static-charged clouds threatened to smother all visibility and electrocute anything that dare enter. Through the flashes of lightning, Captain Bones stared out into the storming sky. There was something else out there with them. He immediately reached to his side and gripped the bone hilt of his sword, quickly unsheathed the sharp silver blade and then pointed it high into the air, bellowing at his crew,

"At the ready!"

Indeed, there was something out there in the storm. Six Reapers raced towards the ascending ship. They flew swiftly and cut through the raging storm with their blood red scythes. Their black oily wings staining the sky and darkening everything in their wake. The Reapers quickly reached the belly of the flying ship and burst into the Knucklebone.

A loud bell rang throughout the ship to warn of the intruders. Captain Bones let loose from the wheel and effortlessly leapt down onto the main deck of his ship. The Skybogs below did their best to slow the Reapers down as they savagely tore through the bottom of the Knucklebone. They were much too powerful and the tiny Skybogs were easily dispatched by their scythes.

The Reapers ripped through the ship and exploded up onto the main deck where Captain Bones and the rest of the Skybogs were readily waiting to greet them with an array of weaponry. The

Reapers did not hesitate and attacked, swinging their blades, splashing oil and fire across the ship deck.

The Reapers suddenly merged together and became an incredibly massive Reaper. It slammed its fist against the blade of the now massive dripping scythe and sent a powerful shock wave across the ship that knocked out every single Skybog still alive. The Reapers disbanded and quickly surrounded Captain Bones. Still, he showed no fear.

One of the Reapers confidently approached him, its burning skeletal face burning mere inches away from his, its black flames singeing his long silver hair and beard as it stared down at him with its empty and hollow eyes.

Without hesitation, Captain Bones shoved the blade of his sword up and through the Reaper's skull. The Reaper grabbed his wrist, burning him with its dark fire, and then slowly pulled the blade down out of its head. It gnashed its teeth at him, grabbed him by his coat, and pulled his face to its skull, but he did not flinch.

Suddenly, Captain Bones was thrown up into the air. From under its exposed rib cage, one of the Reapers thick oily chains shot up and violently wrapped them around his entire body, tightly squeezing as they twisted around him. Then, the six Reapers dove off the ship and flew back out into the storm with Captain Bones dangling below.

Chapter Thirteen: In the Hands of Creation...

Deep in the Underground, Landon slept under the cover of the twinkling lights. After Landon recovered from the crystal ball and his vision, he and Jake conjured up a bunk bed that was long at the bottom, for Simon, and grew exceptionally smaller towards the top where the Halloweenies slept.

Emanating from the bunk above Landon, Sweet Tooth's loud snoring and soft singing made for a restless night's sleep. It felt like only minutes before he heard an eerie voice calling him to wake up as a cold hand pushed down on his entire chest. Landon opened his eyes and jumped at the sight of Simon waking him.

"Stay back!"

Landon tried to stop the words from coming out of his mouth but they were spoken. Simon removed his hand and immediately backed away, lowering his head. A drip of guilt trickled into Landon's veins and flooded his heart. His logic tried to overpower the feeling by combating it with sensible thought. In the end, the war left him riddled with confusion and his sense of compassion consequently yearning to correct his reaction with a meaningful apology.

"I'm sorry, Simon. I... it's just... I didn't sleep very," said Landon, trying to explain as quickly as he could.

"The first ray of the sun has dawned. We must go," Simon said softly.

Landon felt his heart sink into his chest. He then turned and looked out onto the room. He was instantly drawn into a beautiful sunrise and found the room had been replaced with another magnificent garden.

The giant bunk bed sat perched at the edge of a grassy knoll that felt incredibly soft under Landon's feet. The sun rising was enormous, but it did not burn Landon and he could stare right at it without being blinded. The pink ray fell over the cool grass and warmed his skin. For a moment, his mind was completely silent and clear as he watched the sun rise.

Landon put his shoes and socks on and then walked with Simon to join Jake and the rest of the Dreamers. They climbed down the side of a lush cliff to an extravagant playground nestled within a golden field that was surrounded by thick maple trees. There were giant swings and steep swirling slides that the Dreamers were playing on. A gentle breeze kept the falling red and yellow maple leaves floating through the playground like a snow globe after it has been shaken. Pumpkins were lined up around the bottoms of the trees and tiny little gnomes, dressed in various Halloween costumes, were carving them and singing.

As Landon and Simon walked through the playground and past the maple trees, they came to another cliff. They walked up and peered over its edge, only to find darkness. Simon immediately pushed Landon back. He lifted his right hand and ignited a bright purple fireball which he then threw out into the darkness.

The fireball quickly died after it left Simon's hand, but gave enough light to show a large concrete room. Colorful lights twinkled from strings above on the ceiling and began to illuminate the room as they had done the night before. Simon turned back to

Landon and watched with him as the garden disappeared and the room returned to its normal concrete structure. A loud thump could be heard as Frank, who happened to be next in line to go down the swirling slide, fell down and landed flat on his back as the garden disappeared. Madam Roma coughed loudly, looking at Landon and Jake, and asked,

"Now, can either of you pretend?"

"Yes," Landon answered.

Madam Roma placed Landon's hands in hers, leaned in close, and softly whispered something into his ear. Landon smiled and then closed his eyes and began focusing. The room was quiet and dripping with anticipation. The Dreamers had gathered all around Landon and watched excitedly. Landon cleared his head and began to picture the room. He could see the lights and the table in the distance. Then, he pictured himself walking over to the table and saw that there was something upon the table. It was hazy at first, but the closer he got, the clearer it became. Upon the table was plates full of waffles and pancakes, dripping with peanut butter and strawberry jelly. There were large glasses with various juices filled to their rims and steaming pots of potatoes with vegan cheese. Stacked on a silver tray were rows upon rows of vegan tacos loaded with black beans, peppers, and avocado. The aroma made his mouth water.

"That will do, Landon," said Madam Roma, breaking his concentration.

Suddenly, Landon's head filled with pain. His sight dimmed and his body felt heavy. Landon collapsed onto the floor. His head felt as though it had been struck by lightning. Madam Roma placed her hands upon his head and instantly fell onto the ground next to him. Simon raced to them both and picked them both up into his long arms and cradled them until the pain dissipated and both Landon and Madam Roma regained their composure.

"I felt...I felt his pain," Madam Roma whispered.

"Are you okay?" Simon asked.

"Yes. But... "

"But, what?" Landon asked, still holding his head as it lightly throbbed.

"Only a child's Dreamer should be able to feel their pain."

"What does that mean?" Jake asked.

"I do not know."

Simon helped them both up onto their feet, making sure they could both stand on their own before letting go. Landon felt his stomach growl. It suddenly occurred to him that he had not had anything to eat since the previous day. As they gathered around the table and began to examine what had been created, Landon stared at a mess of food slopped into a towering pile. Jake scrunched his face up as he pulled an old brown boot filled with half cooked oatmeal, smelling of sour milk, out of the pile of food.

"What happened?" he asked nasally, pinching his nose closed.

Sweet Tooth grabbed the boot out of Jake's hand, pulled back the collar of his sweater, and stuffed it in where his mouth would be.

"Delicious!" said Sweet Tooth happily, as he slurped down a boot string.

"Um...this isn't what you really eat, is it?" Mad Jack asked.

"Not at all," Landon answered, shaking his head.

Frank reached his thick arm out and grabbed a blackened banana. He then attempted to put the unpeeled banana in his mouth, but the Halloweenies quickly jumped onto his shoulders and took it away from him. Madam Roma rounded the table, placed a hand on Jake's shoulder, and asked,

"How about you try?"

Landon was happy to let Jake try as his head was still slightly throbbing and was in no rush to feel that pain again. Jake sighed and then closed his eyes and started picturing all of his favorite breakfast foods. He was focusing so hard that he looked like he was going to pass out from holding his breath too long. Suddenly, the table creaked loudly and Landon saw it start to wobble. The table started to bow as though something too heavy to be on it was causing the table to warp. The legs started to splinter but still, nothing had appeared.

Landon turned to Jake, who now had a large vein bulging from his sweating forehead. And then, with a huge exhale of held breath, Jake relaxed and opened his eyes. At that instant, a bright light flashed and the towering pile of food exploded onto everyone.

Landon wiped his eyes and face clear from the food that sprayed onto him. There, sitting on top of the entire table was a large, soggy tortilla with a puddle of cheese and peppers. Landon looked over at Jake and started laughing. Jake smiled,

"That looks nothing like what I was imagining."

"What were you thinking of?" asked Landon, trying to stifle his laughter.

"I was thinking of a bunch of stuff. Mostly, enchiladas. "

"For breakfast?"

"Like you did any better," Jake replied with a wink.

Madam Roma lifted her hands and silenced the room. She closed her eyes and began to focus. Plates began to spring up out of thin air. Various steaming dishes grew from the table and filled the air with an aroma that made Landon start to salivate. In mere moments, the table was completely sprawled with an array of amazing food.

While they ate and enjoyed the delicious spread, they laughed about the previous attempts, shared a few stories, and answered each other's questions. All participated except for Madam Roma, who seemed more content in listening than speaking. It was only after everyone had finished eating before she spoke again.

"This ability to Pretend will help you on your journey. Both of you must learn to let your thoughts be relaxed and free flowing. Then, when you begin to flow with your imagination, I believe, you will be able to create anything. Now, before you all leave, I would imagine that you may want to be prepared. Is there something you think you need for this journey?"

"Yes," Landon answered after thinking for a moment.

Landon closed his eyes and began to let his mind wonder. This time, he did as Madam Roma instructed and did not try to control his thoughts or picture anything. Instead, he waited for something to appear. His mind felt clear and grow spacious. And then, an image developed from the blank canvas. It was Alexia. They were standing together in the hall at school, in front of the gym. He could feel the warmth of her smile flow through his body. It made him feel flush with nervous excitement and vulnerable.

Suddenly, her face became dark and his vulnerability was immediately overwhelmed by fear. Landon's body became cold and stiff. Panic swept through his thoughts. Her teeth became sharp and silver and her eyes started to burn wildly with green flames as her skin melted away. Alexia became Vyle.

In his mind, time slowed to a crawl. As he watched the two burning eyes, he suddenly felt drawn into the slow dancing flames. It was then that something began to make sense. For a moment, in the fire, he could still see Alexia's eyes. He no longer felt afraid. Landon felt his fear fade, taking in a deep breath of air and filling his lungs. He reached down to his hip, wrapped his fingers around

219

the hilt of a sword and pulled it free from its scabbard. The hilt was silver and gold with tiny rubies spiraling around it. The blade was glowing red hot with blue flames dancing upon its surface. The sword felt warm in his hand but did not burn Landon. He raised the glowing blade in front of him and watched as the Vyle's wretched body peeled from Alexia like ash caught in a strong wind. Alexia smiled.

After recovering from an immediate burst of pain in his head, Landon opened his eyes and held his hand out in front of him. There, in his right hand, he held up that very same sword. The room was silent as he raised the blade over his head and cheered. Madam Roma winked and then the group rallied around him and joined in to admire the sword. Even though is head throbbed with pain, Landon was too excited about the glowing sword to care.

"Now, what is Death's Hand?"

Chapter Fourteen: The Rule of Thirteen...

"Death's Hand is the tree you saw in your vision. In the beginning it was a syde, planted and grown by Sefryt," Madam Roma answered.

"Syde?" Landon asked curiously.

"It's a seed from the Root," Jeckles interjected, clearly enthralled by Landon's question.

"What is the root?" asked Landon.

"Another great question in which, I know the answer," said Jeckles proudly as he rolled over to Simon and climbed up onto his shoulder.

"It all starts with love. Before the Root, there was only space. In that space there were two beings created by The Great Imagination. The first to be created was 'Enma'. The Second was Rasdem."

"Since the day of their creation their love for each other, just like their lives, became and always will be eternal. To celebrate that love, they were given a single gift from The Great Imagination, a powerful gift known as 'The Seed of Thought'. They were instructed to plant the seed in a special place of their choosing where it could blossom."

"Enma and Rasdem searched for many moons to find the perfect space in which to plant the sacred seed within the new canvas of existence. It is said that where the seed was planted, there are no words to describe the beauty. But, when Enma and Rasdem found the perfect place to plant the seed, Enma held a secret buried deep down within her that The Great Imagination bestowed upon her."

"As much as it pained her, she did as The Great Imagination requested and planted the seed with Rasdem. However, before they planted the seed, Enma cut a sliver of bone from her own spine and then carved it into a ring that she gave to Rasdem to always remember how much she loves him. Then, together they planted the seed into a magical space of wonder and beauty," Jeckles explained as he switched from shoulder to shoulder as if he was performing upon a theater stage.

"But, at that very moment, when shell cracked for the seed to sprout, she vanished. Enma did not exist anymore. In fact, she became, Death. As Death, she is forever bound to rule the realm where all living beings go when they pass away called, 'The Veil'. As for the seed, well it instantly became an omniscient being we call, the Root. The Root is this fabric of existence!" said Jeckles with a nice dismount and a bow finishing with,

"And, I thank you."

"I have a question. Why did Enma change her name to Death?" asked Jake.

"I simply love your brain!" shouted Jeckles as he tapped his cane excitedly.

"This is by far the simplest of answers. Death is how her name sounds when spoken in the first language of the universe," answered Jeckles happily.

"Because that makes sense," said Jake.

"Sefryt went to the Root and stole a syde. He then secretly planted Death's Hand in a place where the weight of time has no pull. I believe the Luminescent Stone is hidden in Death's Hand." Madam Roma finished.

"The what stone?" Jake asked.

"It is one of seven magical stones of Rasdem, the first and most powerful Sandman."

"Yeah, and can totally wipe out every single Nightmare, ever!" Jeckles quickly added, winking at Landon and Jake, coolly shooting at them with finger guns.

"These stones, when together, resonate with everything in all existence. The Luminescent Stone is brighter than any star and eliminates all darkness within its light. All seven of these powerful stones once harmonized within the temple of Efil, birthplace of all Sandmen. Each one, containing its own power over the universe. There was a battle between Rasdem and his own shadow, Sefryt," Madam Roma continued.

"Sefryt?" asked Landon.

"Sefryt was the first being to be created by Rasdem. In the absence of his love, Rasdem suffered a terrible melancholy that consumed him and tore at his being more than any pain imaginable. He took all his sadness and his pain and created darkness. That darkness was his shadow, Sefryt."

"Sefryt was his equal in every way, but at his core... hate. For many ages they created and balanced the universe. Until one night, Sefryt created something completely evil. Rasdem locked Sefryt away in his own hellish creation and left him to rot. And, rot he did, his hate growing, making him stronger."

"Eventually, Sefryt broke free and came for Rasdem. It is said that Rasdem destroyed Sefryt, gave the Root the stones to hide, and then disappeared. For years there have been rumors and whispers of each stone's location, but none have ever surfaced. I believe your vision may be the key to finding the Luminescent stone."

"This stone, it can stop Vyle?"

"I believe so."

"Then, we have to find it. It may be the only way we can save Alexia and Roger. I feel this could be a perilous journey ahead," Madam Roma whispered to Landon.

"For now, let us enjoy our breakfast."

As they ate, Landon turned and explained to Jake how he felt to just let his mind wonder. He told Jake that it was like walking a dog without a leash and how the dog had wandered away from him but never ran away. Landon's acceptance of letting his mind lead revealed an understanding of how to begin creating. With this knowledge, Jake tried to conjure up his favorite chocolate and peanut buttercup candy, but only managed to make bite-sized versions of it, which to him was still a success.

A thought crossed Landon's mind as he watched Jake happily munch on the small candies. Each of these Dreamers had been created from a child's imagination. This much he knew already. Landon had created Simon, but what about the other Dreamers? Were they ever called upon by their children and if not, what happens to them? Landon turned to Jeckles and waited until he finished his treat before asking,

"Jeckles, what happens if a Dreamer isn't called upon by their child?"

"Such an exquisite and inquisitive mind! Well, they simply stay here in Nod. They work in the city and live in the city they were born into or some might move to other Dreamer Cities and make a new life there. Like your world, we have jobs and lives we lead," replied Jeckles.

"So, you make money and go out to eat and stuff?" asked Jake.

"No money. Our world has a much different system than yours. We have more than enough resources. We simply do what we can as a community and work together for the betterment of all our kind."

"You told me when I first got here that you were Simon's mentor. Was that... is that your job?" Landon asked.

Jeckles rolled up into a ball and perched himself once more upon Jake's shoulder and took a piece of his candy. Jake frowned at Jeckles but, allowed it as he too was intrigued to hear the answer to Landon's question.

"Well, I guess you would have found out, eventually. My job was to be Simon's mentor, but now, I work in the games department within the Fountain of Dreams. Anyway, I was assigned as his mentor because... well... " said Jeckles, trying to figure out the best way to answer the question, switching from shoulder to shoulder on Jake.

"Okay look, every Dreamer, when they are born, is assigned a mentor. It's a job that can only be given to a Dreamer that was called upon by their child. These Dreamers, or 'Mentors' would have had full and wonderful days of playing games and sharing secrets with their child."

"Mentors are vital in guiding new Dreamers and teaching them what to expect, things they can do, and the rules every Dreamer needs to know from the moment they are born until the last moment of their final night with their child."

"What do you mean by 'final night'?" asked Jake, looking up at Jeckles.

"Well, mate. When a child reaches the age of thirteen, they are no longer physically able to see their Dreamer. So, that is when that Dreamer will return to Nod and from that moment on, they become 'Mentors'."

"As for the child, their Dreamer becomes an ever-fading memory that slowly disappears as they become teenagers and eventually adults. To that child, that Dreamer simply becomes, what your world refers to as, an 'Imaginary Friend'. Usually recognized as just a phase of their childhood."

"See, the magic that is shared between a child and their Dreamer creates a small light inside of the child. It will never die and it will continue to grow. It will always be pure and always healing. That special light is what their Dreamer gives them to gain the confidence that they need to grow and heal any emptiness they feel in their being as a child."

"That emptiness is what calls a Dreamer to their child. To heal that space is a Dreamer's sole reason for existing. Every single one of us want nothing more than to meet and inspire our children. Some of us are lucky enough to do just that."

"But, sometimes it is a very short-lived experience. Because, at the stroke of midnight, on the child's thirteenth birthday, that Dreamer becomes invisible and there is a shift that child moves into that fades the memory of their Dreamer and allows them to move onto their next transition of growth."

"I will be thirteen next Halloween," said Landon worriedly.

"Halloween!" yelled Lynn and Anne, who then immediately jumped on top of the table and danced happily around in circles.

"So, you were Simon's mentor? That was your first job, right? That means, your child thinks you're only an imaginary friend now?" Landon asked.

Jeckles eyes swelled with tears. Landon looked around the table and felt his stomach tighten at the sight of all the

Dreamers' sad faces. Simon reached over and pat Jeckles on the back of his round head as he blew his tiny nose on Jake's sleeve, then turned to Landon and answered for him,

"Jeckles is actually the only one of us that was ever called upon by a child. The rest of us, except for me of course, did not get called upon or have not yet met their children."

"It's true. I became Simon's mentor because I got to meet my child. But, she... she doesn't think of me as an imaginary friend," said Jeckles, choking back his sobs and then once again, blowing his tiny speck of a nose on Jake's sleeve.

"What happened?" Jake asked as he tried not to be disgusted by the snot on his sleeve.

"Her name was Nina. She liked to be called, Nine. It was her favorite number. She had a tumor in her brain and the day after her ninth birthday, she passed away when the doctors tried to remove it."

"I can still remember when my ring changed. It was her birthday. I was so excited. The day had finally come. My child needed me! So, I ran straight to the Fountain of Dreams and entered the closest Endindrium and traveled to her. When I came out the other side, I found Nine in a hospital room. I saw her sitting on a bed and she was crying."

"When she saw me, she just hugged me for a long time. She told me she was afraid and asked if I was an angel. I told her my name and all about me and where I came from. I remember making her laugh, doing funny impressions, and playing charades."

"I stayed with her through the night. I never left her side, even when the doctors put her to sleep in a special room. I stayed right next to her throughout the entire surgery. She never woke up." Jeckles finished, wiping the tears from his round face.

Then, he rolled up into a ball and rolled over to Jake's chest, who then gave him an awkward hug. Jeckles dried his eyes and once again used Jake's sleeve to blow his nose before he climbed back up onto Jake's shoulder and sat on him like a child would on their parent's shoulders.

"You remind me of her," Jeckles whispered down at Jake, his eyes tearing and his face scrunched at the sadness of Jeckles past.

"It is time. Simon, take them to the stone path of the Maharaji Desert. That is where your journey to finding the stone begins," Madam Roma interrupted and with a wave of her hand, a bright gate appeared at the edge of the large room. With another wave, the table and everything on it disappeared. Madam Roma reached into her pocket, looked up at Simon, and with a wink, handed him a small blue pouch. Simon nodded and then one by one they entered through the gate and left the Underground.

Chapter Fifteen: The Strangest Dreamer...

Once more, Landon stood in an alley. Only this time, there were no shadows. As Landon looked around, he noticed this alley was wide and short. He looked up and noticed both buildings were hunched over and sleeping. These two buildings were leaning so far over and allowed so much light into the alley that it made Landon a little nervous about being seen.

Simon was the last to exit from the gate. And as he did, the radiant gate disappeared. Simon motioned to move to the cover of a wide red dumpster at the end of the alley. The group crouched awkwardly behind each other and hid behind the dumpster. Suddenly, the dumpster spoke.

"Hey, Simon," it grumbled in a thick Australian accent.

"Hey Benny, how are we looking?" Simon whispered to the talking dumpster.

"Everything is pretty quiet around here. You should be able to get out without any notice, mate. Oh, and by the way, I saved you a long coat that someone threw at me. Can you believe it? I still get mistaken as a common garbage dumpster. Look at how immaculately clean I am!"

Landon and Jake took notice that Benny was extremely clean and that he also smelled of soft vanilla and warm sugar cookies. In fact, the awkwardness of how they were all stacked on top of each other was lost in the wonderful aroma that was Benny. Meanwhile, Simon stretched his long arm up and reached into the garbage bin and retrieved a long tattered brown overcoat.

"This is prefect Benny. Thanks," Simon whispered.

Simon put the coat on, stuffing as much of his long wild hair into it as he could and then popped the collar up to hide his face. The rest of the Dreamers gathered into a circle around Simon and the boys as Jeckles explained how they were going to get out of the city.

"Obviously Simon, you know the drill. Sweet Tooth, you make sure that Mert is ready to go," said Jeckles.

Sweet Tooth sniffed his big nose and then casually walked out from behind Benny and around the corner of the sleeping building.

"Okay, now when I say go, we are all going to run onto Mert. Boys, keep low and stay in the circle," Jeckles whispered.

Landon and Jake crouched down inside the circle and waited. Then, Sweet Tooth peeked around the corner and gave two thumbs up.

"Go!"

Instantly, everyone started running together. Landon and Jake kept as low as possible as they ran next to Simon. They had to sprint just to keep up with his long strides. The group ran out of the alley, around the corner of the sleeping building, and down the street. It wasn't long before the circle slowed down and then came to a halt. Landon looked up and saw a crooked sign above the circle with the name Mert written on it. Suddenly, the circle opened and Simon ushered the boys forward to a bus. It was the same bus that Landon and Jake had seen earlier with the giant bee stinger on its end.

"Hurry, before anyone sees you," said Simon as he pushed both boys up onto the bus and followed directly behind them.

"Okay everyone, strap yourselves in! As for you two," said Jeckles, pointing at Landon and Jake.

"Stay down!"

After they found their seats, Landon watched as everyone quickly fastened their seat belts and followed in doing the same. Simon sat across from the boys, who were squished between Mad Jack and Frank, huddled next to each other trying to stay hidden. Landon looked up towards the front of the bus and noticed there was no driver.

"There's no driver?" Landon whispered to Simon.

"Mert is the driver."

Simon crouched down as low as he could and gave a thumb's up to them. Then a loud voice echoed through the cabin.

"Everyone good to go?" said the loud disembodied voice.

"Let's do this, Mert!" said Jeckles who then pounded the window twice and then buckled in.

"Show time!" shouted Mert.

It was the bus, that was speaking to the passengers. Before Landon could ask what was going to happen, the bus became airborne. Landon's body was thrown back and his stomach floated. The bus swiftly raised up into the sky and then flew, wildly darting around buildings and flying Dreamers.

"Won't somebody see us in here?" Landon yelled to Simon.

"We are going too fast. All they can see is a blur. Mert is the fastest bus in the city, maybe in all of Nod!"

"Fastest there is, was, and ever will be!" shouted Mert, making Landon's ears ring.

Jake grabbed his belly. His cheeks puffed, and he felt sick. Landon saw this and immediately pushed Jake's face away from him, just in time to avoid a streaming neon yellow spew of chunky vomit from pouring out of his nostrils and spraying from his mouth.

"That's alright. I got it," shouted Mert.

Suddenly, the windows dropped and the rushing air raced through the bus. Before Jake's vomit could hit the floor, it was sucked out of the window.

"Happens all the time," said Mert and then shut the windows.

"Here comes the fun part. Hold on!"

The bus suddenly did a nose dive straight towards the ground. Landon wanted to close his eyes but couldn't. He could see the road getting closer and closer and felt his heart racing. Jake screamed and gripped the seat as tight as he could. The bus came to a complete stop and hovered momentarily with its nose inches away from the road and then dropped onto its wheels.

"Last stop, The Maharaji Desert!" Mert shouted happily.

Jeckles and the rest of the Dreamers unbuckled their seat belts and, one by one dizzily exited the bus. After ensuring that the coast was clear, Simon motioned to the boys to follow. Landon and Jake exited the bus and once more returned to the middle of the circle. Simon stopped at the foot of the stairs before exiting and rubbed the ceiling vigorously. Mert laughed, and the bus flopped up and down on the road.

"Thanks, Mert," said Simon as he exited.

"No problem, Simon," said Mert as he revved his engine and then once more darted up into the sky and disappeared back into the city.

Simon and the boys stayed low within the circle as the Dreamers guided them to a safe spot within another small garden. It was full of swaying trees and lovely singing flowers. Once Jeckles gave the sign that everything was okay, the circle disbanded and Simon stood up to stretch his long limbs. Jeckles turned to everyone and pointed out at a gate in the distance.

"We are going to that gate. It leads to the Maharaji Desert. Everyone understand?" asked Jeckles.

The group nodded in agreement and waited for Jeckles to give the order to go. Landon could see the gate beautifully sparkling as it sat snuggled within a gigantic brick wall. Simon looked up to the sky and noticed that the second sun was already receding from its highest point. They did not have very much daylight left.

"This is it. If you want to back out, now is the time," Simon whispered to the Dreamers of the group, but no one moved.

"No, Simon. We are all going with you," said Sweet Tooth.

As they all moved to the edge of the garden, something caught Landon's eye. There was somebody walking towards the gate. He tugged on Simon's tattered sleeve and pointed and whispered,

"There's somebody coming."

Everyone stopped and watched as the mysterious figure, shrouded in a long flowing burgundy robe with a hood covering its head and concealing its face, slowly walked across the street towards the dazzling gate. As the figure walked, Landon could hear the sounds of metal clanking with each step the figure took.

"What's he doing out here? He never comes out!" whispered Jeckles as though seeing a ghost.

Jake pushed his way up next to Jeckles and, with no regard to hiding his voice, asked,

"Who is he?"

Mad Jack slammed his giant paw against Jake's mouth and hissed,

"Be quiet!"

Jake shrugged and kept quiet as they watched the shrouded figure stop for a moment as though he had heard Jake. The figure tilted his head towards the garden they were hiding in as he paused for a moment, then turned back to the gate and resumed walking towards it.

"That's Stilts. Nobody really knows anything about him, except that his name is Stilts," Simon whispered to Landon and Jake.

"Nobody, I mean, nobody, has ever seen his face," Jeckles whispered.

Landon watched as Stilts reached a crystal hand out from under his robe and gently traced his beautiful fingers down the center of glittering doors.

"He doesn't talk to anyone and likes to be alone. I can appreciate that," said Simon.

"I heard from some of the mentors that his child met him and did not want him to come back. That his child was scared of him and forbid him to ever see him again. So, he could never return and has stayed hidden in that big cloak he wears," squeaked Sweet Tooth.

Landon watched as Stilts placed his crystal hand back under his robe and then slowly turned away and walked back into the city.

"What was the point of that?" Landon asked.

"Who knows," whispered Mad Jack.

"He am shinny like door. Maybe he am related to sparkle door!" said Frank proudly.

"Maybe, Frank. Alright, now everyone follow me," Jeckles whispered and motioned for all to follow.

They quickly ran to the sparkling gate, following Jeckles in a circle around Simon and the boys. Jeckles popped up at the gate then rubbed his small fingers across the glittering poles, making it sing and then open just like the one that the boys had entered to get inside Reflection City. This time however, there was no blinding light behind the gate doors, just a warm breeze rolling off of a calm and motionless red desert. One by one they entered through the gate and left Reflection City.

After exiting the gate, Landon turned around only to see the city was no longer behind them. The city lights he had seen light the sky so brightly had completely disappeared. Only a glittering golden gate stood upon the red sands of the Maharaji Desert.

"Well, this is the path that Madam Roma told us to follow," said Jeckles as he flicked his cane and tapped it onto a sparkling stone road leading out into the red desert.

Lynn and Anne climbed up onto Mad Jack, who had laid down upon the warm stones and was purring under the rays of the setting suns. This made it incredibly easier for the Halloweenies to climb up and ride on his back after he was finally convinced to walk. As they followed Jeckles down the path, Simon walked between Landon and Jake, trying to shorten his long stride so they did not have to sprint to keep up.

After a while, the road became wide which allowed everyone to walk next to each other. No one spoke for a while and Landon could tell that they were all in a vigilant state of mind with the disappearing light fading fast. Simon kept his only eye on the desert while the rest of the Dreamers cautiously walked next to him.

"Why are you all so quiet?" Landon asked.

"We have never been on this side of the city walls, out in the Maharaji Desert," Simon replied.

"There are stories of creatures called 'Nocnistas'..." Simon tried to explain but was interrupted by Jake who asked nervously,

"What are Nok Knee Stahs?"

"They're tiny blue-haired hags and they eat Dreamers. Apparently, they live out in the gray swamps not too far from here and are loyal to Nightmares. The Nocnistas give them shelter from the light, allowing them to travel from Nyx and attack Reflection City," said Simon eerily.

Landon and Jake immediately searched the desert for any kind of movement.

"What exactly is does a blue-haired hag look like?" Landon asked.

"Well, I have heard that they look like tiny old ladies with blue hair and lots and lots of wrinkles. Oh, and that they have tiny cottages that smell like pies and after they lure a Dreamer to their home, they eat them with their rows and rows of tiny sharp teeth!" said Sweet Tooth in a soft frightened tone.

"No, no, they look like tiny old men from a distance. Real fragile and weak. That is, until you get close and they transform into giant scaled worms with rows and rows of giant razor-sharp teeth. They live in caves under the swamps and drag Dreamers down into them to eat them!" said Mad Jack as the terrified Halloweenies on top of his back hugged each other.

"Stupid old man ladies! Frank hate worms. Frank like tiny snails with nice shell house," Frank shouted.

Simon stopped walking, which made everyone else stop and become silent, and then he pointed ahead.

"There is something moving out there in front of us."

Landon squinted his eyes and tried desperately to see, as did everyone else, but he could only see waves of heat rising from the desert floor.

"What does it look like?" Jeckles asked, rolling himself up onto Simon's shoulders.

"I cannot tell. It just keeps bouncing around," Simon replied.

Landon immediately recalled the large bird he had envisioned back in the Underground and walked faster down the road.

"I think that is the bird I saw in my mind."

"Wait, Landon!" Jake yelled and ran after him.

Simon took a few steps and caught up to Landon. He reached down and picked both of the boys up and placed them on his shoulders, causing Jeckles to jump off and roll next to him. Eventually, they reached a fork in the road and there stood Krawk, a giant purple-feathered bird that Landon had seen in his vision. Krawk seemed to take no notice of them standing before him and repeatedly hopped around, slamming his beak into the sand.

Simon helped the boys down from his shoulders and waited for the rest of the group to catch up. Once they did, Simon had to stand in front of Mad Jack, whose eyes became dilated and stalked the giant bird's every movement.

"Jack, stay back!" Simon warned with a harsh tone to his eerie voice, snapping his long fingers loudly, catching Mad Jack's attention.

The snapping sound made Krawk stop hoping and stand straight up. The giant bird twitched and his feathers ruffled as he looked upon the group. His movements were sharp and fast, with two black beady eyes blinking rapidly as his head tilted in new directions constantly.

"Hi, my name is Landon. what is your name?"

"KRAWK!" shrieked the bird.

"Um... Krawk?"

The giant bird hopped quickly towards Landon and pointed his small green beak at his face. Krawk tilted his feathered head, stared into Landon's eyes, and then screamed in a shrill voice,

"KRAWK! Yes, I am Krawk!"

The Dreamers had now helped Simon by forming a barrier between Mad Jack and Krawk. Mad Jack was licking his lips and digging his claws into the ground below as he watched the giant bird bounce around. Before Landon could ask him anything, Krawk had once again resumed slamming his beak into the ground.

"Krawk, can you help us? Do you know where to find Death's Hand?" Landon asked, but the bird did not respond.

Once again, it was as if they were invisible. Suddenly, Simon remembered the blue pouch that Madam Roma had given him. Simon retrieved the pouch and handed it to Landon.

"Try this."

Landon untied the pouch and opened it. It was full of small pink wriggling worms.

"Ew!"

Landon hesitantly reached into the pouch and grabbed a handful of the pink worms. They felt slimy in his hand and slithered between his fingers. He then approached Krawk and tossed two worms onto the ground. Krawk stopped hopping and slammed his beak down at the worms inching across the sand. He devoured them in seconds and then, when they were all gone, he stood straight up and hopped back towards Landon.

"More? More! KRAWK!"

Landon held his fist forward as if to drop them onto the ground and watched as Krawk hopped back and waited, his focus never leaving Landon's hand.

"Krawk, I need to ask you some questions. If you answer them, I will give you these worms, okay?" Landon said, dropping a couple onto the ground.

"KRAWK! Yes. Questions. Worms. More please. KRAWK!" screeched the giant bird.

"Krawk, I need to know where to find Death's Hand. Can you tell me where it is?"

Krawk's beady eyes stalked Landon's fist as if he was hypnotized. He flapped his little wings excitedly then tilted his head and answered.

"Yes. KRAWK! Worm?"

Landon dropped two more wriggling worms onto the desert road and waited for Krawk to finish eating them before asking him another question.

"Where is Death's Hand?"

Jake felt his stomach wrench and turn as he watched Krawk slurp down another worm.

"Bosque De Los Muertos, KRAWK, must go into the forest of the dead, forest of bones, KRAWK!"

"Forest of bones? Anyone ever heard or know where the... 'Bosque De Los Muertos' is?" Landon asked the group.

Everyone looked around at each other with questioning faces. It was clear to Landon that nobody did. So, once more he grabbed a fist full of worms, held them out in front of Krawk, and asked,

"How do we get to the Bosque De Los Muertos?"

Krawk hopped around, his feathers became ruffled and he puffed up like a balloon. Then, with a loud screech he responded,

"Follow the right road, KRAWK! Follow until the sleepy comes. KRAWK! Fly in the twisty, KRAWK! See the bones, hear the clatter!"

Krawk seemed to get agitated and pecked at Landon's shoes. Landon dropped a few more worms, hoping this would calm him down a little.

"One last question, Krawk. Then I will give you the whole bag," said Landon, opening the small pouch and showing Krawk the pink worms sliding over each other inside of it.

Krawk stopped pecking at Landon's shoes and stood completely still and focused on him.

"Is there anything in the forest that can hurt us?" Landon asked.

Krawk tilted his head and blinked rapidly. For a moment he said nothing. Then he chirped until his chirps became an excited answer.

"Yes, Tribu De Los Muertos. KRAWK! Worm?" he replied.

Sweet Tooth ran over to Landon and tugged on the knee of his pants so hard that his pants sagged and he had to quickly pull them up.

"I have heard of them. The Tribe of the Dead! They never sleep, eat anything or anyone they come across, and worship Death," whined Sweet Tooth nervously.

"You mean, like, cannibals?" Jake asked.

"Do cannibals eat Dreamers?"

"I guess they would," Jake answered.

"Then, yes. They are cannibals," Sweet Tooth replied.

"Ouch!" Landon interrupted, feeling a sudden sharp sting to his hand, turning to see that Krawk had pecked at him trying to get the bag.

Landon turned the pouch over and all the remaining worms fell onto the ground. Krawk danced around happily, pecking at the ground, vigorously swallowing the pink wiggling worms. By this time, everyone had forgotten about Mad Jack, who was now hunched down and ready to pounce. His eyes still dilated and fixed on the giant bird. Mad Jack licked his lips and then suddenly sprang into the air, leaping over their heads and diving straight down at Krawk with his fangs and claws ready to attack.

"Jack! No!" screamed Jeckles, but it was too late.

Mad Jack slashed at Krawk, but to his surprise, Krawk was incredibly fast and dodged his every attempt to catch the bird.

Krawk became a whirlwind of pecking chaos and pecked at Mad Jack savagely. The tables had turned and Mad Jack was on the run, trying to get away from the giant puffy bird. He retreated and ran behind Frank and hissed. As the giant bird approached, Frank grabbed Krawk and smacked his beak, pointing his thick finger and scolding the bird,

"Bad burdy!"

Krawk turned around and scurried off into the desert, picking up the bag of worms as he ran. As he darted off into the desert, it looked to Landon as though he were trying to fly but his wings were obviously too small to lift him up into the air.

"Jack, you're such a wimp!" said Lynn, petting his paw while he moaned obnoxiously and licked at his tiny wounds.

"The first sun has set. We need to hurry," said Simon, pointing a long finger up the last sun.

The group agreed and hustled down the road. Even with night quickly approaching, they kept their spirits up with the continued ridicule of Mad Jack and how quickly Krawk was able

to defeat him.

Chapter Sixteen: A Pirate's Life...

"Welcome." said Vyle.

Captain Bones felt his knees slam against the wet ground and a sharp pain slice through his shoulders as a Reaper dug its claws into him. His long silver mane of hair hung down over his face, making it hard to see who was speaking as the Reaper shoved his head down. It didn't matter, Captain Bones knew exactly where he was and even worse, who was speaking to him.

"What do you want with me, wretch?"

The Reaper's claws stabbed deeper into his shoulder and even though he could feel the sting of his flesh being sliced into and the warmth of his blood running down his arm, he did not make a single noise. Vyle crouched down and with a long silver claw, lifted Captain Bones' chin up until his face was parallel with Vyle's burning eyes and his wet grin.

"I want to tear the flesh from your bones and dangle you on a painful edge of life before snuffing your light!"

Then, with a closed fist, Vyle back handed Captain Bones across his face and knocked him to the ground. Before Captain Bones could get up, the Reaper had grabbed him and once more forced him to his knees.

"But alas, you are not afraid. You are the man without fear, aren't you? You're nothing to me but an empty dinner for a starving horror!" screeched Vyle as he rose and paced.

"A man..." Vyle whispered.

"In the land of Nod? No, I think not. Your eyes tell me that much. Perhaps, a Dreamer then? No. You stay far from the Dreamers. What then?"

Then, Vyle crouched back down and once again put his monstrous face directly in front of Captain Bones' now bleeding face. He stared sinisterly into Captain Bones red eyes. Vyle snarled as his eyes burned brighter and brighter. Captain Bones was caught in the Nightmare King's stare as if hypnotized and then the white around his red eyes filled with dark smoke until all that was left was black. As Vyle stared into the darkness of Captain Bones' eyes, he searched to reveal his secrets that had been buried within his mind, but Vyle only found a dark abyss of emptiness.

"What are you?" Vyle growled.

As Vyle searched Captain Bones' empty eyes, the fearless man spit on the Nightmare king's pale tightly stretched face. Vyle laughed wickedly as he stood up and then he kicked Captain Bones right in his mouth, splitting his bottom lip open. The blood ran down his silver haired chin. The split in his lip burned badly but Captain Bones kept smiling and chuckled as he spit the blood from his mouth onto Vyle's feet.

"What do you want?" he asked.

Vyle snapped his silver claws and two Reapers flew past him into the darkness behind the Nightmare King. Vyle stood above Captain Bones quietly staring down at him and watching the blood drip from his mouth as he waited for the Reapers to return.

It only took the Reapers a few minutes to return to Vyle. As they flew out from the darkness, Captain Bones saw that each of them carried a frail looking child chained to their ribs. Captain

Bones could see one was a boy and the other a girl. The Reapers threw the children carelessly down in front of Captain Bones and pulled their chains painfully tighter as Vyle traced his claws over their heads.

"A child, in Nod," Vyle snickered.

Captain Bones grit his teeth and sprang up from the ground but was immediately slammed back to his knees. Vyle grabbed the children by their heads with his sharp claws and turned them towards him. They screamed in agony as he cut into their flesh and laughed while Captain Bones watched in horror as he fed from them. The Nightmare King drank in their fear and drained both of the children until they became frail and limp. Never once taking his eyes burning emerald eyes off Captain Bones as he fed.

Captain Bones watched the life of both children drain into Vyle as their bodies became skinny and pale. Their hair grayed and their skin wrinkled. When Vyle had reached his fill, he tossed their limp bodies to the ground.

"Delicious!" Vyle roared.

"Now Captain, you will bring me the child I am seeking."

"And, if I refuse?" said Captain Bones, clenching his jaw and staring up at Vyle.

Captain Bones turned his angry eyes down at the limp children lying on the wet, cold ground. He could feel his heart become heavy. He turned his eyes back to Vyle's.

"I know you have been searching all of Nod for something. Something dear to you. Something close to your pathetic heart. Something or maybe... someone? Bring me the child and I will give you this."

Vyle smiled wickedly as he reached into a small bag made entirely of smoke. He revealed a spy glass from within the bag. The spy glass was silver and wood with jewels and beautiful symbols carved into it. The crystal was black and made the spy glass impossible to see through. Captain Bones eyes widened, and he involuntarily jolted up towards the spy glass but was retrained by the Reaper behind him.

"Interestingly enough I know that it only works for you too," sneered Vyle as he looked it over. "I also know that this has something to do with finding what you are looking for. Bring me the boy and it is yours once more."

Captain Bones felt the Reaper lift him up off of his knees and place him back onto his feet. Vyle stood over the frail children and smiled as he stared at their limp bodies.

"Tell me Captain, what shall I do with these?" Vyle asked, motioning to the two waiting Reapers to take the barely breathing children away. Captain Bones said nothing and spit on Vyle's face.

Vyle and Captain Bones laughed then he grabbed Captain Bones by his throat and lifted him up off the ground into the air, choking him and cutting his skin as he dangled.

"Not a man. Not a Dreamer," Vyle sneered.

Then, Vyle dropped Captain Bones and with the snap of his fingers, the Reapers once more wrapped Captain Bones' body in their chains and wrenched him up into the dark sky above. As he ascended into the frozen clouds, Captain Bones wrestled his hands free from the strangling chains. He then reached into his shirt and retrieved a small skull made from a dark meteorite that glittered in his fingers. It was decorated with rare jewels and precious metals with intricately carved symbols attached to a silver chain around his neck. With the skull in between his fingers, Captain Bones flicked open a tiny latch. The skull was actually a secret locket.

Captain Bones held it carefully in his fingers and stared at a small picture inside. The picture was of a smiling young girl. Gritting his teeth, he put the tiny photograph back in, closed the skull locket, and tucked it back into his shirt. With pure and absolute hatred burning within his eyes, he looked down upon the rotten wasteland and whispered,

"I will find you."

Chapter Seventeen: Into a Skeleton Forest...

Walking through the desert had taken most of the day and the last warm rays from the second sun fell upon Landon's face as the continued to wander down the road.

"Here we go." said Jake uncomfortably.

The thought of being out in the open desert in the dark made everyone uncomfortable.

"Gather around in a circle." Simon ordered.

Quickly they formed a small circle as the last rays of the second sun fell and disappeared below the horizon. Darkness drenched the desert like a swift rain flooding the land. Suddenly, the road beneath their feet glowed brightly.

"What's happening?" screamed Jake as he bent over and wrapped his arms around Jeckles.

Jeckles felt just as nervous but couldn't help but smile up at Jake and feel a little joy that he was holding onto him. It inspired courage in him and he felt proud and strong. A savage tornado of red glowing dust smashed into them and swept the group up into the swirling cyclone. Landon closed his eyes to keep from getting dizzy but he could not escape the feeling of his body being violently whipped around by the angry winds. He turned to see the Halloweenies desperately trying to grab onto each other to stay together.

A Jack-o'-lantern trick or treat pail flew directly towards Landon and smashed into his nose. His nose burst with blood and his eyes instantly watered. He then blindly reached his hands out and managed to pull Anne into his chest, who was clenched in a ball to keep little Anastasia from coming out of her pocket. Lynn however, was spinning too wildly to reach Landon and went flying right past him. Anne screamed, trying to extend one of her little arms out to catch her but Lynn had disappeared into the tornado.

Above Landon's head, Simon's long arms bolted past him and snatched up the panicking little Halloweenie. Simon reached and pulled Lynn into his chest just as the tornado abruptly stopped and they were all thrown to the ground. There were many groans of pain and a lot of confusion as they picked themselves up and regained their footing.

"You're safe now." said Simon as he placed Lynn down gently onto a thick gray grass.

"Thank you." said both Halloweenies simultaneously to Landon and Simon.

Then, the two Halloweenies immediately ran over to each other and talked so fast that nobody could understand what they were saying except each other. Simon opened his hand, and made a small purple flame appear to light the way, then turned to Landon and whispered,

"We must be silent and keep our eyes open. Nightmares could be anywhere now that it's dark."

The group gathered once more and explored the visible land around them. Landon unsheathed his sword and used the light from the blade to help Simon as he looked for a path. Jake took notice of Landon's softly glowing sword and sighed.

"It's the sword, right?" whispered Landon.

"Everything I make comes out wrong, man. I want a cool glowing sword or something. But, if I try to make something like that, I know it's just going to come out crappy," Jake answered, feeling defeated.

"I was going to ask you once nobody was around if..."

"Just try, man. Close your eyes and let your mind wander like I told you. Release your control and glide into the flow." Landon interrupted.

Jake took in a deep breath, then closed his eyes and scrunched up his face as he tried to focus on creating his on weapon.

"Jake, you're already trying too hard. Just relax and let your mind drift."

The group had now stopped moving and instead stood around in a circle watching Jake as he tried again. Jake's eyes closed once more and this time his mind filled with random images. He found himself standing in his homeroom at school. The lights were off and the room was empty. It was eerily quiet, and the air smelled burnt. Then, from outside the classroom, Jake heard the sounds of someone crying faintly echo through the hallway.

Jake left the room and entered the dark hallway but this hallway didn't look like the one in his school. This hallway was tall and crooked. The lockers were old and rusted and the paint was peeling from the walls. Fear crept up behind him like a cold stalking shadow as he walked through the empty hallway. Then, in the darkest shadows at the end of the hallway, he saw a little girl sitting on the floor.

"Are you okay?" he said and heard his voice echo in different tones down the hall.

The crying stopped and the little girl stood up and started to twitch as she walked down the hall towards him. Her movements were not like the way a normal person would walk, they were sharp, jagged, and fast.

The hall became cold and Jake felt his heart race. The girl ran at him and scream. Her screams dropped Jake to his knees and felt like they were burning his ears. Jake felt his body stiffen from a paralyzing fear as he watched the little girl transform into a wretched clown with hideous teeth and two big knives for hands.

As the horrible clown neared, Jake took in a breath and tried to remember what Landon told him. Clarity washed over him and replaced his fear. Then a bright red light engulfed him and freed his body.

Jake looked down at the floor and saw a magnificent hatchet burning brightly with red fire dancing over its razor sharp black blade. As it burned brighter and brighter, the hatchet hovered and gently float into the palm of his reaching hand. The flames were burning hypnotically. Jake was mesmerized by its beauty. The hatchet rested comfortably in his hand. Its weight was perfect. Its metal hilt was smooth and dark with several red stones embedded into it and the burning blade formed one long black fang at the bottom of the blade's fiery edge.

Careful not to focus too much on the hatchet, Jake stood up and faced the approaching clown that filled the hall with horrific screams that pierced his ears. Jake swung the fiery hatchet through the pain and watched the blazing glory of its blade smash into the heart of the clown. Instantly, an explosion of white light tore through the darkness and blinded Jake. He opened his eyes to see he was lying on his back and immediately felt a sharp sting at the bottom of his spine.

"My ass… "

Just as he was about to get up he saw something burning on the ground next to him. It was the fiery hatchet he had imagined. He grasped the hatchet in his hand and lifted it up to see.

"Whoa!" said Jake in awe.

"That is so sick!" Landon whispered excitedly helping Jake up onto his feet.

Suddenly, Jake dropped the burning hatchet and fell back down onto his knees. He breathed heavily while grabbing his head, grunting as the piercing pain temporarily overwhelmed him.

When Jake regained confidence in his ability to stand on his own, he was so impressed by what he created that he could barely take his eyes off of the glowing hatchet, swinging it around while he made his way through the dark. After a little wandering

Jake raised his hatchet up and found a dense white forest swaying in front of him. He turned back to the group and said in a somewhat hushed voice,

"Um... guys? I think I found the Bosque De Los Muertos."

Standing before all of them, was a thick wall of bone white trees. Landon took notice as the wind blew around the group and made everything near them sway and rustle, except for the forest, which didn't make a sound.

"Simon... Are we really going in there?" Sweet Tooth asked reluctantly.

"Yes."

"That's what I thought. Oh dear..." Sweet Tooth whispered as he gathered the collar of his oversized sweater and pulled it up over his nose, trying to hide everything but his eyes so he could see.

One by one, they squeezed themselves through the strange thick trees. Upon entering the forest, Landon placed a hand on one of the trees and felt its surface. It was smooth and cold. It didn't feel like any tree he had ever felt before. All the leaves had fallen off and lay motionless upon the ground. It was as if the forest was dead.

"Simon, check this out," Landon tried to whisper but to his surprise, there was no sound.

Simon however, turned around and approached Landon as though he heard him. Confused, Landon tried to ask,

"Can you hear me?" but once again, no sound came from his lips.

"Yes, I can hear you," Simon answered, but his voice sounded different.

It sounded like it came from within his head. Landon motioned for Simon to shine his light on the tree and look at it.

"Is this bone?" Landon whispered in his head as he rubbed the tree.

"I think it is,"

Landon heard Simon's voice ring through his head again and felt a little dizzy as it flooded his brain.

"Do you hear that?" asked Simon.

Landon turned and listened but did not hear anything.

"Hear what?" Landon answered.

"That's just it,"

"I hear nothing. Look," said Simon in Landon's head, pointing at the group as they made their way farther into the forest.

There was no rustle from the dead leaves they stepped on and not a single sound from within the forest. Landon couldn't even hear himself breathe.

"Jake!" Landon tried to scream, but again no sound came from his mouth.

"How is it that we can hear each other?" Landon asked.

"I don't know?" Simon replied.

"We can totally talk to each other without even having to speak out loud! Cool," said Landon in his head.

Simon and Landon then caught up with the group and quickly gathered them together. It only took a few moments for everyone to realize that they could not speak to each other and that there was not a single sound to be heard around them.

Jake closed his eyes and pictured a handful of pens and tiny note pads. After a tiny shock of pain subsided, the pens he tried to create turned to crayons and the tiny note pads had become sticky notes but they worked just fine for relaying messages to each other. Landon and Simon decided not to tell everyone what they discovered. Landon believed it might upset the other Dreamers.

The group stayed close, keeping all eyes on each other and on the forest, until they reached a small clearing where they made camp for the evening. They knew it was too dangerous to be out in the dark, so Landon and Jake collaborated on creating a cabin that would house and protect them through the night.

Together they breathed in deeply and focused on a drawing they had put together in order to picture the same things. As their minds wandered, they pictured the cabin resting in the clearing under the moonlight. It took a couple tries for the two of them to work together, along with the fact that the pain would interrupt their focus, but after their third attempt they had created the cabin. However, it did not look like the one they had drawn.

Standing before them was a tall and large concrete box with one giant circular door and no windows. Its roof was the only thing that looked like it belonged on a cabin. Landon and Jake both shook off the lingering pain in their heads and then entered their creation with the rest of the Dreamers.

To their surprise, the inside looked exactly like a wooden cabin, complete with a roaring fire and several beds. The beds all had pillows and blankets and sitting in the center of the room was a table filled with food. Everyone tried to express their happiness, but still no sound could be heard. So, they just smiled at each other and ate.

Landon explored the large cabin and found a strange mechanism attached to the latch on the inside of the circular door. Landon pushed down on a silver button and witnessed three thick steel rods slam across the back of the door and lock the door securely in place. Then a large spotlight placed above the entrance beamed directly on the entire door. Landon grabbed Jake, pointed to the light, and without speaking, asked if that was his idea. With a mouthful of food, he nodded excitedly and gave a thumb's up and then took a moment to marvel at it before returning to the table and stuffing his face.

After eating and once again checking that the only door to the cabin was secured, everyone climbed into their beds and fell asleep. All except for Simon who sat by the fire as it burned warmly and stretched up out of the huge fireplace. The smoke climbed up through the chimney and freed itself from several small holes in a thick iron cover secured on the top of the chimney. As the beautiful smoke danced magically over the cabin and up into the star riddled sky, it was suddenly ripped through by the belly of the Knucklebone as it sliced through the night, soaring over the Bosque De Los Muertos, searching for Landon.

Chapter Eighteen: Here Time Stands Still…

The flames in the fireplace had calmed and its soft orange and red embers glowed warmly. All was still and more than silent. Not a breath or a snore could be heard from the sleeping Dreamers or the two boys. They all rested comfortably and drifted into the beauty of dreams.

Landon sat down at the dinner table in the kitchen. Moira, who was faced away from him, was cooking something on the stove while Jensen, who was sitting across from Landon, flipped through a magazine that hid his face.

"Hello son, how did you sleep?" Jensen asked, also speaking in an odd sounding tone.

"I had a bad dream." Landon replied.

"Did you have a nightmare?" Jensen asked loudly as he quickly flipped through several pages of his magazine.

Landon became more than a little unsettled by the sudden loudness of his father's voice and hesitated in the continuing conversation. But alas, answered his father's question.

"I... I don't remember."

"You don't remember*?" Jensen yelled abruptly, slamming the magazine so hard down onto the table that the glass cracked.*

Landon immediately noticed that the man sitting across from him was not his father. Instead, it was a man dressed like him that didn't have a face. Landon jumped up and backed into a corner in the kitchen.

Suddenly, the room become cold and he could see his breath. Landon quickly looked to his mother as she turned around, revealing she did not have a face either. Then, before he could move, the lights flickered, and the kitchen shook.

"How could you forget!" she yelled, making all the windows and the glass table shatter.

Landon jerked up from his bed, opened his eyes, and searched the surrounding room. After realizing that he was safe and that he had been dreaming, his heart beat slowly returned to normal. Landon took in a deep breath and shook off the odd dream, but he was not relieved to be in Nod. As Landon looked around, he noticed something strange. The cabin walls and only the walls were all gone. Everything else, however, had stayed exactly the same.

"Good morning," said Simon in Landon's head.

"Good morning," Landon replied a little startled as he got out of the bed.

Together, Landon and Simon woke everyone up from their slumber. After ensuring that there were no intruders lurking around the edge of the clearing they had slept in, they enjoyed a small breakfast. Landon and Jake had little difficulty creating things now and quickly became skilled at creating food. The second sun would soon rise and the group knew they needed to get moving. Once more, they all entered the forest even though none of them knew where they were going and what to even look for.

They trekked long and far, hoping to see some kind of sign to point them in the right direction, but with every step the forest just grew deeper and thicker. Landon stopped and, with Simon's help, rounded everyone up.

"We need to come up with a plan." Landon wrote on his little paper.

"We can't just keep walking and hope to find Death's Hand. We need to figure out what we should do."

Everyone agreed, but no one offered any suggestions. What could they do? There was no path and nothing that Krawk had told them gave them any idea about where to go. Landon stared at a group of bone trees as he waited for anyone to chime in with an idea and then it hit him.

"Simon, give me a boost. I'm going to climb up this tree." said Landon in his head.

Simon lifted Landon up onto a thick bone limb of the closest tree and watched as he quickly climbed up high above the group. Landon scaled the tree until he reached a branch that offered him the best view to see the forest in all directions.

The sun was so bright it made his eyes water. Landon quickly placed a hand upon his brow, shading them from the light. Once his eyes adjusted, he looked out over the vast forest. Miles upon miles of the leafless bone forest stretched out into the horizon. As he turned around, to look behind him he saw plumes of red smoke rising from the forest. Oddly enough, Landon could hear the faint sounds of an engine grinding over the rattling trees swaying in a wind. He also heard the branch he was perched upon start to crack and hastily scurried back down to the group below.

One by one, they took turns climbing up and seeing the red smoke. They all agreed that it could be where Death's Hand is and set out to find it. They walked for hours, pausing only to climb a tree every now and again to regain their bearings. As they journeyed deeper into the forest, Landon felt the Halloweenies climb up onto his shoulders and Mad Jack's soft fur rubbing against his arm.

Then, just as the first sun began to dip behind the trees, they reached a clearing. The group quickly took cover behind a cluster of trees and saw a massive stone temple that looked extremely similar to the Aztec pyramids that Jake visited with his family last summer on vacation in Mexico. From the top of the temple, rising above the forest, were the red plumes of smoke. And floating right over the temple, was the Knucklebone.

As Landon looked over the floating pirate ship, he could see the Knucklebone's massive metal gears rotating and grinding, streams of hot steam whistled and spewed from various pipes and green fluid dripping as it flowed through hundreds of thin tubes weaving in and out of the ship. Squinting his eyes to focus, Landon noticed several canons and small shadows haunting the circular windows lining the ship's side. He quickly returned to the group to find that Jeckles had taken Sweet Tooth and the Halloweenies to search the perimeter. After ensuring that they were alone and agreeing on the safest path to the temple, they slowly made their way down into the clearing.

Once they reached the edge of the clearing, they cautiously stepped free from the trees, out under the second sun. Landon and the group approached the temple. As they got closer, Landon saw an opening at the base of it. Suddenly, a loud wail broke the silence and pierced through their ears like a sharp needle. Landon howled in pain and fell to the floor. Simon tried to reach over and cover Landon's ears but it was too late. The painful sound dropped everyone to the floor. A group of skeleton warriors quickly tied them up and lined them out in front of the temple.

The Knucklebone quickly descended, landing next to them as Landon and the rest were sat down on the ground. Captain Bones exited his ship with a number of Skybogs and promptly made his way to Landon and the restrained group. Gathered around them like a pack of starving wolves, was a tribe of sinister looking skeletons carrying various sharp weapons. Many of them had long spears with enormous black feathers tied to them while others were armed with bows and arrows or brutal double-edged blades.

The skeletons wore thick furs and decorated themselves with disturbing trinkets and jewelry that had been made from the teeth and small bones of rodents and birds. They also had incredibly detailed symbols carved into their skulls that were painted in a shade of red that could only be blood.

Landon suddenly felt his head being lifted. A skeleton grabbed his face and stared into his eyes with its hauntingly hollow eye sockets. This skeleton differed from the rest as it wore a thick feathered headdress with several tiny animal skulls and a few red stones set into a rusting metal crown that was holding the long black feathers. This skeleton must be their leader.

"Chief Ratanrok, do you have what I came for?" boomed Captain Bones, who was now standing behind Landon.

"We tracked them from the moment they entered the forest. There are two," answered Chief Ratanrok

"I'll take them both."

"We keep the Dreamers," Chief Ratanrok snapped, pushing Landon's head back and chattering his teeth as turned his attention away from him and over to Captain Bones.

"Look at me, boy," Captain Bones ordered Landon.

"Why are you here?"

Landon said nothing. Captain Bones raised his hand and then slapped Landon across his face. Simon twisted and attempted to lunge at him, but he was still tied down and unable to move.

"Why are you here?" Captain Bones asked again and still he said nothing.

"Hit him again and I'll kill you," Simon said coldly.

"What if I cut him? Or... " Captain Bones taunted, pulling out a small knife, walking over to Sweet Tooth, and then tracing the cool blade under his eye.

"We... We're looking for Death's Hand," Sweet Tooth squeaked, trembling as Captain Bones stared dead into his big eyes.

"Shut it, Sweetie!" shouted Mad Jack.

"Why?" said Captain Bones, continuing to lightly dragging the tip of the blade down Sweet Tooth's long nose, making him cross-eyed as he followed the knife.

"To find the Luminescent stone!"

"Luminescent stone? Kill them all, NOW!" Screamed Ratanrok, attacking Captain Bones.

Captain Bones pulled out his sword, prompting his Skybogs to do the same, and defended himself against the deathly Chief. Signaling to one of his Skybogs, Captain Bones yelled,

"Cut them free! Take them to the forest, wait for me!"

A tiny Skybog, wearing pair of bright pink pants, smiled and began bouncing around, dodging slashes and stabs from the skeletons trying to kill him. The tiny Skybog slide under a low swinging blade, over to Landon and the group, cutting them free and then pointing to the forest and yelling

"Follow me!"

Without any hesitation, Landon and the group bolted for the woods, following the tiny Skybog into the tree line with Captain Bones hot on their trail as the tribe of rattling skeletons, hurling spears and shooting arrows at them.

"Call the Gnashers!" screamed Chief Ratanrok.

A skeleton perched at the top of one of a tree retrieved a long bull horn from his belt and then blew into it making a noise that howled above the darkening forest. As Landon and the group ran, a trembling roar shot out through the forest. The Trube De Los Muertos fell to their knees and worshipped with sounds of bones rattling and teeth chattering.

"Quickly, this way!" yelled Captain Bones, grabbing both Landon and Jake and darting off into a new direction.

"Landon!" yelled Simon, his hands burning brightly with purple fire as he and the rest of the Dreamers immediately chased after Captain Bones.

The forest roared and violently shook as an icy wind sliced through the rattling tree limbs. Something was coming towards them and it was moving fast.

"What's that noise?" Landon yelled.

"Something bad," Captain Bones answered.

The ground shook harder and the thundering sounds of trees snapping grew closer. Landon reached for his sword but before he could pull it free, he suddenly became weightless. He was now falling backwards down into a dark hole that Captain Bones had thrown him and Jake into. As he fell, Landon watched Captain Bones get violently tackled into the hole by Simon with the rest of the Dreamers diving in immediately after them.

Landon felt his body smash into the ground below and all the air forced out of his lungs. As he desperately tried to breathe, Landon could hear Simon and Captain Bones and quickly rolled out of the way just as they came slamming into the ground. Immediately following them were the rest of the Dreamers, who came tumbling recklessly down onto each other.

Jake picked himself from the ground and pulled his hatchet from his belt. The blade's hypnotic flames lit the dark tunnel around them and revealed Captain Bones standing close by with his sword drawn at the ready to attack Simon, who was now standing in front of Landon with his fists burning wildly. The rest of the Dreamers quickly joined Simon's side and formed a barrier between Captain Bones and the boys.

"I am not the one you need to protect them from!" Captain Bones shouted angrily.

"Frank don't like you. Me am going to smash your head. Rock!" said Frank, holding up a large boulder over his head.

A loud roar came directly above the dark hole they had fallen through as something monstrous tore through the forest and shook the ground they stood upon. They all stared up into the dark hole and waited. After a few moments they heard another roar, but now far off in the distance.

"Keep quiet!" Captain Bones whispered.

"Gnashers! This be the only place in this forest safe from Gnashers." said Captain Bones, sheathing his sword and withdrawing from his fighting stance.

"I'm scared, what's going on? Are you going to hurt us?" Sweet Tooth asked faintly.

"Let him try!" hissed Mad Jack.

"Calm yourself, little Dreamer. I won't hurt you," Captain Bones replied.

"Explain yourself!" demanded Jeckles.

"Vyle, wants one of them," Captain Bones answered, pointing at Landon and Jake.

"We already know that," said Simon.

"But, the Luminescent stone… " Captain Bones said, staring deeply out into nothing.

"It can end all of this."

"All of what? What are you talking about? Why are we down here?" Jeckles angrily asked.

"Death's Hand," Captain Bones answered.

"Lord Vyle, him and his wicked Nightmares… he is so powerful. The torture he brings to Nod, to children… he kills them. All of them. The Luminescent stone, if its real, can stop him from ever hurting another child again and I know where to find Death's Hand."

"Why do you care about who he kills?" asked Simon.

"What are you anyway? You're definitely no Dreamer. Where did you come from?" Captain Bones asked, pointing up at Simon.

Mad Jack pounced onto Captain Bones, pinning him to the ground and hissed,

"He is a Dreamer!"

"I'm simply curious, ya big fur ball. Just never seen a Dreamer like him. Now, get off of me!" Captain Bones shouted.

"Don't let it happen again." said Mad Jack.

Then, he deliberately turned his furry body around on Captain Bones' chest with his tail lifted up over Captain Bones' face before allowing him get back up.

"And, he is from Reflection City like the rest of us Dreamers," Jeckles added.

"Reflection City? Never been, but I met a Dreamer from there a while back. Saved her from a pack of Nocnistas. Nasty creatures! Rows and rows of tiny sharp teeth."

"I told you!" whispered Sweet Tooth to Mad Jack.

"Doesn't prove a thing!"

"How come we hear each other now?" Landon questioned.

"Yeah, what was that all about?" Jake questioned.

"It's nothing special, just a hunting spell that the tribe's Shaman placed on the forest. Anything that enters, loses the ability to hear. makes hunting a hell of a lot easier. Once you come into contact with any members of the tribe, the spell is lifted," answered Captain Bones.

"Now, we don't have too much time. Soon the Gnashers will track us."

"For crying out loud, what are Gnashers?" Jake asked, raising his hatchet farther into the dark.

"They're enormous beasts with huge teeth, poisonous claws, and breathe fire. More importantly, they will kill anything alive in this forest. Just think of them as big and terrible wolf dragons," Captain Bones answered.

Suddenly, a tremendous rattling echoed through the darkness all around them. Bright flames lit up the darkness as they saw the Trube De Los Muertos, led by Chief Ratanrok, running towards them. The world slowed and once more Landon found himself in a trance of time, moving like snowflakes floating down a still wind.

"Everybody take cover!" Captain Bones growled in a deep and distorted voice.

Landon watched beautiful sparks of a burning fuse dance upon the wick of what looked like a metal grenade being thrown out of Captain Bones hand as Simon pulled him down to the ground. He slowly fell with the rest of the group, watching a single spark fall with him, which was actually a tiny fire fairy smiling and waving up at him.

Landon felt the sudden impact of hitting the ground and time return to normal as he and the group fell behind a cluster of rocks just in time to avoid being ripped apart by a giant explosion of metal shrapnel and purple flames. The skeleton bodies were ripped to pieces and sent splinters of bone flying all across the cave and right into the palm of Landon's hand, wincing in pain as the bone stabbed into his soft flesh.

Landon looked down at his palm. A long thin sliver of bone had buried itself deep into the center of his right hand. He reached over and pulled the splinter out and then tossed it angrily away. Landon felt the warmth of his blood drip through his fingers and quickly applied pressure with his left hand to stop the bleeding.

"Follow me. Quickly!" Captain Bones yelled.

Captain Bones ran into the darkness and the group followed. They ran until Landon could see a light shining down from an opening in the ceiling of the cave onto the giant roots of an enormous bone tree. The massive tree and had many thick limbs with blood red leaves waving upon its swaying finger tips. It was the biggest tree Landon had ever seen.

"Death's Hand," Landon said in awe.

"Yeah, kid. That's why we are down here. Now climb!" shouted Captain Bones, pointing to the opening in the ceiling.

"Why are you helping us?" Landon asked.

"You really want to know that now? Kid, believe it or not, I am not a big fan of Nightmares and from what I hear, that stone can kill them."

As Landon and the group followed Captain Bones up the gigantic bone tree, the blood from his hand dripped down onto several elegantly carved symbols that covered its entire pale surface and made them glow a soft red light.

"Interesting…" said Captain Bones as he reached down and pulled Landon up.

Captain Bones lifted Landon up onto a flat and perfectly circular landing and then did the same for the rest of the group. Simon was the last to climb up. He had ensured that the Halloweenies and Sweet Tooth made it up the gigantic tree with him. Once Simon reached the landing, he saw they were all staring down at the landing.

Carved upon the surface of the landing were three large circles. The first and largest of the circles wrapped around both the second and third circles. And the second circle, just like the first, wrapped around the smallest and third circle. Within each circle, flowing slowly around the carvings, was a clear liquid. Landon knelt down and then submerged his bloody hand into the clear water to wash it off. Suddenly, the clear water began to spin and glow a bright red.

"What's happening?" he asked.

"I'm not sure," Captain Bones whispered.

Landon pulled his hand out of the water and quickly picked himself up off the ground. The circle not only became very bright, but it started to spin rapidly. Landon looked over his shoulder and saw that Simon was standing right next to him.

"I'm here," said Simon reassuringly.

Suddenly, the glowing liquid shot up into the air, forming a floating red glowing ring. The second ring glowed and did the same as the first. Then the third as well until all three glowing circles were floating and spinning in the air above their heads.

Then, the glowing circles stretched and form into a perfect glowing sphere. The sphere spun and quickly shrank down into a tiny bubble that floated down onto Landon's palm. There was a brief pause, and all was silent as everyone watched the bubble come to rest upon his bloody hand. Then, the small white bubble burst, sending a massive shock wave out that knocked everyone to their knees. When they got back up, Landon was kneeling on both knees with an iron box sitting in his hands.

Landon cautiously pulled up on a small silver latch to unlock its grasp and then carefully opened the iron lid. Instantly, the whole cave became blindingly bright. There was not a single spot of darkness or trace of a shadow to be found anywhere. Through the blinding light, Landon heard Simon's voice,

"The Luminescent Stone."

Chapter Nineteen: The Root and the Journey...

The entire cave was bathed in a brilliant white light. Every

shadow had been destroyed from the vibrant rays of the

Luminescent Stone. As Landon reached into the box, he noticed

that the wound on his right hand had been completely healed. He

then reached down into the iron box and retrieved the bright stone.

As he held it in his hand for everyone to see, Landon saw that what

he was holding was actually a small black ring with a beautiful

blue sapphire stone fastened to it that was emitting the brilliant

white light. Oddly, the light did not hurt any of their eyes with the

exception that Simon squinted behind his eye piece.

"After all these years spent following whispers in the wind

and shadows of half-truth. I believed the 'Luminescent Stone' was

just a story." said Captain Bones as he stared wide eyed upon

Landon and the ring.

Landon paced for a moment and then turned to Simon,

handed him the closed box. Simon took the box and unlatched the clasp. He then opened the lid and picked up the ring, but nothing happened. Landon reached out towards the ring and the stone glowed. He quickly pulled his hand back and then pointed for Simon to hand the box over to Jake.

"See if it glows for you," said Landon.

Jake took the ring, still it did nothing, even after putting it on his finger and shaking his fist. Still, nothing happened. Jake then put the ring back inside the box and closed it and handed the box back to Landon.

"So, what do you think that means?" Landon asked Jeckles.

But before Jeckles could respond, the cave echoed with unsettling sounds of rattling.

"We need to leave, now!" shouted Captain Bones.

The splintered remains of the Trube De Los Muertos pieced back together. Captain Bones jumped up onto a low hanging branch and climbed with the group right on his heels, all except Landon, struggling to climb as he tried to carry the iron box up the tree.

"Ditch the box, kid!" shouted Captain Bones as he pulled a black scarf off his belt and handed it to him.

"Here, wrap it in this."

Landon took the scarf, wrapped the ring, and then shoved it into his front pocket of his jeans.

"Now then, move! Through the leaves!" Captain Bones yelled, pointing up to the opening as Chief Ratanrok and his warriors quickly scaling up the large tree.

"Quickly, my ship is just up ahead of us!"

They each climbed up to the tip of the last limb that was just barely reaching out over the ground above the opening in the cave. And, one by one they jumped off of the limb and landed onto the ground. They were only a few feet from where the Knucklebone was hovering, and as they all made their way to the ship. Suddenly, a terrifying roar rattled the entire forest.

"Gnashers!" shouted Captain Bones.

The Gnashers had picked up their scent and quickly made their way through the forest, straight towards them. The group ran to the ship and climbed up a rope ladder that led up onto the Knucklebone's main deck. Once they were all aboard, Captain Bones shouted orders to his Skybog crew and pulled the rope ladder up before the skeletons below could grab onto it.

The tiny Skybogs immediately took to their posts, released the sails and started the massive engines. As the Knucklebone quickly lifted up into the air, Captain Bones took the group and showed them into his chambers and locked the door.

"It will only take the Gnashers seconds to find us once we leave," said Captain Bones pointed out a window of his chambers.

"The first sun will rise within the hour. We must stay hidden in here, and mask our scent, until the first light shi… "

He was suddenly interrupted by a loud hiss coming from a dark corner of the room. A Reaper had been waiting in the shadows. Captain Bones had believed the Reapers had left after they delivered him back to his ship, but in fact, one had stayed aboard to watch him.

The Reaper's sharp red scythe sliced at Captain Bones' chest but he swiftly dodged the long blade and watched as it sliced down onto a thick wooden desk. Pieces of splintering wood and debris smashed loudly as the Reaper hacked and slashed at them. Landon and Jake drew their weapons out from the cover of their sheaths and stood ready to fight while Simon conjured two fiery fists. Captain Bones slashed savagely at the Reaper, but once more found that every slice or stab had no effect on it at all. Simon shot a purple fireball from his fist at the Reaper, causing it to howl in pain upon impact. Frank flipped the heavy desk over onto the Reaper's chest, pinning it to the floor.

"Bad Nightymare!" Frank shouted.

"Quick! With your flames, light him on fire again!" yelled Captain Bones to Simon.

Simon once more shot the purple fire from his hands and bathed the Reaper in flames. It roared in pain and screamed so loud that it made the glass in the windows explode. The Reaper twisted frantically and pulled itself loose from the heavy desk, leaving its lower half still pinned. Then it dove out the shattered window and plummeted down into the forest below. Suddenly, the room filled with the horrible roar of the Gnashers.

"They're coming," shouted Jake as he saw several fury dragons flying up towards the ship.

"Get to the deck!" yelled Captain Bones.

They all followed Captain Bones and ran out of the room, back onto the main deck of the ship. Captain Bones leaned over the edge of the ship and saw that the Gnashers were gaining on them. Their sharp teeth grinding and their white hair fluttering in the wind like thin needles.

"Ready the canons!" Captain Bones commanded his Skybogs.

The two closest to him saluted and immediately vanished in a small puff of orange smoke. Then the ship's heavy gears began grinding even louder. The windows surrounding the flying ship popped open and several canons stretched out of them. The Gnashers were only moments away from attacking the ship when Captain Bones shouted,

"FIRE!"

"Watch out!" Landon yelled to Captain Bones as a Gnasher dove and grasped its sharp claws onto the Knucklebone.

"You! Can your fire hurt them?" Captain Bones screamed and pointed at Simon.

"Let's find out," said Simon as he ran under the perched Gnasher with both hands burning brightly.

Simon poured the purple flames into the Gnasher's belly. At first, it did not seem to be working but then the Gnasher released its grasp on the ship and fell back down to the forest. Simon continued to keep the Gnashers at bay with his fire as Captain Bones took the wheel.

The Knucklebone's engines whirred loudly as part of the exposed engine shifted and transform. It sprouted three large tubes from the back of the ship's engine. Those tubes suddenly burst with fire and the Knucklebone immediately shot into the sky. All of them except the Skybogs were immediately thrown backwards. Mad Jack had clung to the railing of the back of the ship with his claws, otherwise he would have surely been thrown right off. Landon and Jake were pinned down by Frank onto the wooden floor while Sweet Tooth and the Halloweenies were being held tightly in Simon's arms as he held onto the center mast of the ship. Landon looked up and saw the sun rising as they rocketed upwards. The ship sliced through the clouds, up into a world of radiant pastel colors and twinkling stars.

"Cut the fuel," shouted Captain Bones.

The grinding metal gears and pumping tubes slowed to a halt as the ship powered down. Once it did, it came to a gentle and smooth sail. Landon and Jake looked over the ship, down onto the forest below and saw that the Gnashers were flying away from them.

"We did it!" Jake shouted, causing the entire ship to cheer.

After checking that everyone was okay and assessing the damage of the ship, Captain Bones handed the wheel over to a rather plump Skybog, giving him a wink and a hard pat on the back.

"Turn this ship starboard. We fly south to Nyx."

He then turned to Landon and the group and with a slight chuckle he smiled at Simon and shook his long hand,

"I hope you're all ready for this. That was the easy part."

Chapter Twenty: The Land of Nyx...

The Knucklebone sailed swiftly through the bright and colorful sky. For the moment, all was calm and quiet, except for a beautiful whistling coming from the pursed lips of a green and yellow stumpy Skybog, adorned with military ribbons and medals. Apparently, the little Skybog's job was to serenade the Captain and crew as they soar through the skies of Nod.

Landon became lost in the hypnotic tune, transfixed on the magnificent glittering sky, and drift to thoughts of Alexia. Jake picked himself up from a comfortable nest he made out of some rope and cloth he found on one of the decks below and then walked over to Landon.

"Hey man, I've been thinking," said Jake.

"About what?" Landon asked.

"What are we doing, man? I mean... about Vyle. What's the plan?"

"I'm not sure, but we have to do something right? Vyle has Alexia and Roger. He came after us..."

"He came after you," Jake interrupted.

Landon became quiet, pacing in thought as he imagined what would have happened if he had come home from school alone that day instead of with Alexia, Jake, and Roger.

"You're right. You shouldn't be here. This is my fault. I'll..."

"You'll shut your dirty mouth," Jake jokingly interrupted. "I am going with you, end of story. All I know is that you better have some kind of great explanation for our parents when we get home. And, just know that if I get in any kind of trouble... I'm totally gonna blame you. You know, it we make it out of here alive."

They both shared a weak laugh and then rejoined Simon and the rest of the Dreamers who were leaning over the edge of the ship and looking out into Nod.

"So, now that we have the Luminescent Stone. Does this mean we can stop Vyle?" Anne asked.

"Yeah, does this mean we can kick that no good 'Ug-o' out of Nod for good?" Lynn added.

"I truly hope so," Landon answered.

"Can we see it again?" asked Sweet Tooth softly.

"Certainly," said Landon as he pulled the ring from out of his pocket carefully unfolding the scarf.

A bright light suddenly beamed over the ship, blinding them all. Captain Bones barreled in and quickly pushed the ring back into the scarf as he pushed it back into Landon's chest.

"That is nothing to play with!"

Landon quickly put the stone away. A few Skybogs that happened to be standing close to him were now walking into each other, trying to rub the spots from their eyes. One even fell right over and just laid on the deck, smiling. Another pulled out a pair of sunglasses and gave Landon the finger, staggering off and grumbling. Captain Bones gave a hearty laugh and then returned to steering the ship. Landon then turned to Simon and asked,

"Are you scared?"

"Yes," Simon replied.

"Why are we doing this alone?"

"What do you mean?" Simon questioned.

"Why is there not some army or something to help us?"

"Many live trapped within the grip of fear. They find comfort in their naivety and ignorance. After Dozer was taken, Deity has ordered all Sandmen to return to Efil. There are no armies, just us," Simon answered.

"But, if the Nightmares catch you they will make you one of them," whispered Landon, with a look of deep concern upon his face, starring out at the passing clouds floating by them.

Simon placed his twisted hand on Landon's shoulder and turned him to face the group.

"They will never leave your side. I, will never leave your side."

The group rested for the moment, not hearing Simon and Landon's conversation while Captain Bones however, had listened intently.

"I know of a way into Nyx where we can find the children without detection," said Captain Bones shooting a quick wink up at Simon.

"At the top of Vyle's tower is an unguarded entry."

"Unguarded?"

"Aye! And, there be a good reason for that, kid."

"Figures," Mad Jack growled as he passed by and found a nice empty space to stretch out.

"Won't to be easy. But once inside, we will have a much better chance at finding the children and getting out alive," Captain Bones continued.

"Do you know where to find them?" asked Landon.

"Yes."

"So, how do we get to Nyx if it is under Nod?" asked Landon.

Captain Bones placed his hands behind his back, his eyes transfixed on the horizon with his long silver hair waving in the wind, he answered,

"In my travels, I've crossed over the Eternal cliffs and sailed above the forbidden waters of Nyx. Think of Nod and Nyx as opposite sides of the same coin. To get there, we'll have to go over the Eternal cliffs and then through the forbidden waters," Simon explained to Landon.

"We have to fall off of Nod?" asked Landon nervously.

"Aye! And, be sure to stay out of the water. It's full of monstrous sea creatures so poisonous that even a single drop of their venom will burn right through your bones! As I was saying, I was flying this beautiful ship, which you all are so lucky to be on, close the Eternal cliffs, not far from Del Toro, looking for..." Captain Bones paused.

"For?" asked Landon.

"Lillian," whispered Captain Bones taking in a deep sigh.

"Lillian?"

"Someone I made a promise to. Anyway, my crew and I were caught in a large storm a few years back and it pulled us right over into the forbidden waters. I thought we were all done for. That it was the end for us. Instead, we found ourselves sailing through the black skies of Nyx."

"Black skies? " Jake asked.

"There's no sun, no moon, no stars, no warmth, no nothing. Just darkness. Back to what I was saying, we were spotted and attacked by Nightmares. I remember waking up, chained to a wall, locked in a dungeon. There were children in the dark with me, chained to the same wall. There was this little girl, I could barely see her face, but when I saw her eyes… " Captain Bones took a moment and paused as he restrained his eyes from watering.

"Vyle thought I was a Dreamer, and he tried to change me. When he couldn't, he entertained his filthy Nightmares by torturing me instead. He tried to break me. Didn't work. After he got tired, he took the little girl and ripped her apart in front of me… slowly. Made me watch. Still hear her screams when I sleep."

"After Vyle was done, he took me back to my ship along with a hundred or so of his wretched Nightmares. Brought another child with him, a small boy. Threatened to do the same to him as he did to the little girl if I didn't help them cross into Nod. So, I did and dropped Vyle and his Nightmares to a nasty little swamp, full of Nocnistas, thinking they would take care of them."

"When we landed, Vyle brought the little boy to me, dragging him like a rag doll and then snapped his neck like a twig. I tried to cut his head off, but the next thing I remember, I woke up, buried up to my neck somewhere in the middle of the desert."

"Left me to rot, and probably would have died if it hadn't been for the help from some big dumb bird. I still have the scars from him pecking at me," said Captain Bones angrily as he pulled the collar of his shirt and revealed a few tiny scars on his neck.

"After Del Toro, I went back to Vey. Cost me in more ways than I could have ever known. I found an unguarded entrance at the top of Vyle's tower. I made my way in, all the back to the dungeon. I went to save the kids but… they were all just meat and bones," Captain Bones finished.

The night quickly stretched over the sky as the last sun finally set and the ship approached the Eternal cliffs. Landon stared out into the horizon of stars and planets growing bigger as they flew through the darkening sky. Then shifted his eyes, discovering another brightly lit city below.

There were bright lights and winding roads weaving in and out of rolling hills and tall smooth buildings. To Landon the city below looked like any city he had ever flown over in a plane back on his world.

"That down there is Enetria. The city of stars," said Captain Bones.

"It's also that last city before the Eternal cliffs!" shouted Jeckles as he pointed up at a large storm that seemed to have instantly appeared over them.

"Aye! We are not far now."

"You know, now that I am thinking about it," Landon said, looking over his sword and nodding to the group. "I think they may need weapons too."

One by one the boys created weapons for each Dreamer. They started with the Halloweenies. They each filled their Jack-o'-lantern trick or treat pails with various pieces of candy, each with their own ability. Their favorite being a red round candy that exploded when it hit something. That something was a nearby Skybog butt that Captain Bones convinced the Halloweenies to test it on.

The Skybog screamed, desperately patting the flames out on his little butt. Suddenly, the little Skybog burst into flames. Three lager Skybogs threw him on the deck and quickly rolled him around trying to smother the flames. Captain Bones and the Halloweenies roared in laughter as they watched one of Skybogs come running over, pouring buckets of water with slimy fish over the burning Skybog, who then ate the fish.

"I think he farted," whispered Captain Bones to the Halloweenies.

The three of them stared silently at each other for a moment before erupting into more laughter. Next was Sweet Tooth, they made a pair of red neon tiger claws he could wear on his little hands. He liked Mad Jack's claws and wanted claws like his. Mad Jack apparently approved, as he then taught Sweet Tooth how to swat, slash, and stab.

Mad Jack however, wanted nothing, except another buttered salmon. Then, for Frank, Landon, and Jake made another boulder. Which he tossed from one massive hand to the other as he repeated several times to his boulder,

"You am good rock."

And, for Jeckles, they gave his cane the ability to shoot bright floating orbs. These orbs were like glowing bubbles that produced minutes of bright light as they floated. The Skybogs became instantly amused and watched as many of them tried to catch the bright orbs with their mouths.

"You're next," said Landon to Simon.

Simon produced a purple fireball in the center of his hand and replied,

"I'm good."

"By the way, there's something I forgot to mention..." Captain Bones shouted as a loud roar of thunder erupted through the sky.

"What do you mean, forgot to mention?" screamed Jake anxiously.

Suddenly, a bolt of lightning struck the tallest mast of the Knucklebone. The ship however, was unharmed and actually seemed to gain speed.

"Well, now you know. That happens a lot, so try not to get hit and die. Gives the 'ol Knucklebone' the burst of life she needs to get enough speed to get over the cliffs," shouted Captain Bones, smirking as Jake glared up at him.

A storm quickly consumed the ship and Landon could no longer see the wall of stars and planets. As they sliced through the gray clouds, Captain Bones howled with joy and ordered his Skybogs to take their posts.

Lightning struck the ship again and again and Mad Jack just so happened to be a little too close to the mast, making all his hair stand straight up. This made Frank extremely happy and caused him to shout,

"Fluffy Kitty!"

He was so excited about Mad Jack being zapped by the lightning that he jumped up onto the center mast and climbed to the top, reaching both hands up into the air, and getting himself struck repeatedly. This actually helped the Knucklebone as Frank made a great conductor and gave the ship more than enough speed to break out of the storm and into space.

As the Knucklebone dove over the cliff, Landon, they all held on trying not to be thrown overboard. Landon felt his stomach drop like he was on a steep rollercoaster and couldn't help but smile. Meanwhile, Jake was not having the same fun as Landon and was screaming in a really high pitch.

At the point where Landon felt like he should fall off of the ship, gravity changed and they were immediately pulled back down onto the main deck. Landon felt his stomach return to its normal position and quickly jumped up to see where they were.

He looked out over the deck and saw nothing in the sky but darkness and raging waters below. In the distance, rugged mountains and another storm quickly gaining on them.

"Welcome to Nyx!" Captain Bones shouted. "Now, keep both of your eyes open. This place, everything here will try to kill you. Vyle's tower is just up in those mountains. Once we get there, we will only have a few seconds to get through or else we will all be completely ripped apart. So, when I go, you go! Understand?"

In front of the Knucklebone, out in the distance, Landon could see a terrible storm raining down upon a deadly jagged wasteland. He could also see something spinning and reaching high up over the crooked land into the storming clouds.

"There it is. The Nightmare city, Vey," said Captain Bones with a look of hatred in his eyes.

They sailed quickly over the dark decayed land and over countless crooked buildings that lined the haunting roads of a rotting city. The streets slithered with shadows that played hair raising tunes from clanking metal, creaking doors, and howling winds whistled through broken windows, around corners, carrying wretched whispers as it weaved through the condemned city.

"Take us higher!" ordered Captain Bones.

Slowly, the ship rose into the dark gray clouds that drenched the dark city in freezing bullets of ice and water. Higher and higher they rose through the frozen clouds until the Knucklebone broke free from its grip. As the ship leveled over the storm and under an empty black sky, Captain Bones shouted,

"There!"

Vyle's tower was just ahead of them, piercing through the top of the raging storm, was a massive cyclone, spiraling and violently twisting into the black sky. Jake immediately felt his hand being grasped. He didn't even have to look down to see it was Jeckles.

"When we are close enough, you will see the opening we will drop through. On my order, everyone will jump straight into its center. If you do not fall directly down the center, you will not make it, so say your goodbyes if you have any," ordered Captain Bones.

With that, Captain Bones then gave his Skybogs control of the Knucklebone and prepared for the jump. As they sailed closer, the twisting winds pulled the ship towards the tower until they were less than a foot away from it. The Skybogs raced to keep the ship from being pulled in and torn apart by the violent spinning tornado as Captain Bones jumped up onto the edge of the main deck. As Landon looked over the deck down onto the spinning tower, he felt his heart pound and his breath quicken.

"Get ready!" shouted Captain Bones.

Everyone quickly climbed up onto the ships ledge as the Skybogs ignited the engine and positioned the ship directly above the opening. The ship began to rattle and pieces ripped off into the spiraling wind being sucked up into the night.

"Now!" Captain Bones yelled as he jumped off the ship into the towering cyclone.

Without any hesitation, they all jumped, each of them disappearing into the twisting smoke. Landon looked over to see Simon falling next to him and Jake with Jeckles holding onto his back. Suddenly, a concrete floor appeared. Simon reached over and pulled Landon and Jake onto his back. Simon's feet slammed into the concrete, causing it to crack underneath him. The Halloweenies smashed into Frank which softened their landing while Sweet Tooth had clung onto Mad Jack and kept shouting,

"Cats always land on their feet!"

The group stood upon a mountainous stone tower, safe from the circling wind. And after a quick regrouping they were ready to go. As they ran to the center of the tower, Landon watched the dark clouds spiraling around him. They now moved slowly and gracefully like a calm flowing river. It was completely silent. Not one sound of wind could be heard, except for their breathing. It was almost beautiful.

"Over there," Captain Bones whispered, pointing at a small door off in the distance.

They quickly followed Captain Bones to a large rusted iron door and, with a nod from Simon, Captain Bones pulled the heavy iron door open. The door creaked loudly and echoed down into the abyss of the pitch-black tower.

"No turning back now," Captain Bones whispered, disappearing into the darkness.

Chapter Twenty-One: Staring into the Abyss...

"Ready?" whispered Captain Bones.

"Yeah, everyone ready? I'll just be here in the back," Mad Jack answered, though it was obvious he was afraid.

"Scaredy-cat!" giggled the Halloweenies.

"This way," Captain Bones whispered.

The decended into the darkness, holding up their weapons to see. They found themselves in an empty, pitch-black, stone room. Suddenly, green fire ignited upon the fingertips of the many clawed hands aligned upon the walls and dimly lit the room.

As they followed, Captain Bones brought them to a tall and crooked door that looked like it had been stretched out of shape and buried into the wall. When he opened it, Captain Bones revealed a long black staircase that spiraled down into Vyle's lair.

One by one they made their way down the spiraling staircase, into the foul smells of rotting meat and mold. The stairs were slippery and oddly angled, making it difficult to walk down, except for Mad Jack who heard the clatter of chains and tried to run back up the stairs, but ran into Frank instead and was now being carried down the stairs like a baby.

Landon and Jake had initially noticed that each step did not disappear and therefore felt a little relieved. These black steps however, were like the ones they had fallen off of at Simon's house as they too were not connected to a handrail of any kind, they simply hovered. With each step they took, the black surface rippled like water under their feet, but did not wet their feet nor spill over.

They passed several doors of varying sizes and shapes as they descended deeper into the darkness. Some of them looked like rusted iron prison doors while others were wooden, rotten, and falling apart. There were even a few black holes with the hinges still hanging, nailed into their stone edges.

"We are almost there," Captain Bones whispered.

The sounds of chains clanking faintly echoed from within the darkness in front of them as they each found footing onto a large landing below. Mad Jack's short and normally silky-smooth hair had grown almost ten times in size, making his hair stand straight up and giving the Halloweenies a quite a fluffy ride as they climbed up onto his back.

"Just through here," said Captain Bones, pointing to a large hall that shimmered as if there was a blood red pool of water reflecting from some hidden light in the dark hall.

They cautiously made their way through the giant hall to another crooked door that led them down another spiraling staircase, all they way down to the sub levels of the enormous tower. There, they found Vyle's dungeoun, a large circular room with several iron doors.

"We are here," said Captain Bones.

"Not that I am complaining, but don't you think this was just a little too easy?" asked Jake.

"I'll take the easy way and you take the hard way. Then, let's see who comes out alive, eh kid? Whaddya say?" Captain Bones retorted.

"Hey old man, don't get sassy with me! I have seen a ton of movies and read tens of scary books. So, I KNOW… that this was way too easy!" Jake snapped back.

"Oh, well then… excuse me," whispered Captain Bones sarcastically.

"Okay, well we are here. So, what now?" Jeckles asked, interrupting Jake and Captain Bones.

"Find Alexia, save the children, right? Just keep your eyes open. I'm telling you all… this feels like a trap," replied Jake, looking at Captain Bones with big eyes and then narrowing them suspiciously.

Jeckles mimicked Jake by looking up at Captain Bones, opening his eyes as wide as possible and then narrowing them too. Captain Bones rolled his eyes at Jake and walked over to the door, knelt down, and retrieved a lock pick. In a matter of seconds there was a soft click, and the door was unlocked. Captain Bones smirked as he pulled it open and then entered the dungeon.

Landon and Jake followed closely behind Captain Bones. Each holding out their weapons and shining their lights upon the dark walls of the wet room. Then Jake saw something chained to the wall.

"I think I'm going to be sick," gagged Jake through his sleeve.

Landon peered over Jake's shoulder and saw a rotting corpse. Landon felt nauseated and dry heaved as he breathed in the foul stench. Captain Bones grabbed a torch and traced the light over the rest of the wall. In the corner was a pile of skeletons.

They quickly ran to the pile of bones and searched for signs of Alexia and Roger, but the bodies were far too decayed.

"They're not here," Landon whispered as he choked on the putrid smell surrounding them like a stagnate fog.

"Yeah, I think these have been here for a while." Jake whispered.

"Let's check the others."

The group entered a second dungeon, a third, and a fourth, finding each of them full of decomposing skeletons and still, no signs of Alexia or Roger. Then, upon shining their light into the darkness as Landon and Jake entered the fifth out of seven doors. Suddenly, the silence in the room was broken by a quick rustling of chains slinking across the wet stone ground.

"Alexia?" whispered Landon.

"Alexia, it's Landon."

The rustling stopped. Landon waited and after a brief silence a weary voice spoke from within the darkness.

"Landon?" whispered Alexia faintly.

"It's her! Alexia!" Landon yelled in a hushed voice to the group as he ran over to her.

Alexia was chained to the wall like all the other skeletons they had discovered in the previous cells, but something was wrong. She looked different. Landon and Jake were startled by her appearance. Alexia had become thin and her hair was coarse and gray. She looked old and painfully fragile.

"Are... you real?" she whispered.

"Yes, and we are getting you out of here," Jake answered as Landon waved Captain Bones over to pick the locks of her chains.

"Who... who are they?" Alexia whispered nervously.

"Don't be scared. These are our friends and here to help us all get out of here," Landon assured Alexia while Captain Bones broke her free from the locks and then helped lift her onto Mad Jack's back.

"Where's Roger?" asked Landon.

Alexia's eyes filled with water and she pointed a boney finger back into the darkness of the room. Jake ran to where she had pointed and retrieved his hatchet, shinning the light to find Roger. There, under a pile of ragged clothes and rusted chains, were the broken bones of a skeleton. They were the bones of Roger.

"He's dead..." she whispered.

"That thing... it tortured us... over and over again. It ripped him apart... until all that was left were bones. It ate most of him except the meat from Roger's face. It played with the pieces and then… it… it made me eat his face! It made me eat his goddamned face!"

They all stood silent, shocked at what Alexia had just told them. Jeckles approached her and gently touched her hand. Alexia did not move. She was frozen in the memory. Landon could see she barely had the energy to even lift her head, and that she was growing weaker by the minute.

"My dear, we will get you home. I promise, but I need your help first. We are looking for our friend, Dozer. He's a Sandman, have you seen him? Is there anyone else here?" Jeckles asked.

"Up… up there," answered Alexia, pointing to the stairs before she lost consciousness.

Before leaving to find Dozer, they searched the two remaining cells. They discovered and freed a group of three children in the last dungeon, chained to the wall and huddled together in the dark.

"Who are you?" asked a weak looking boy.

"I'm Landon and these are my friends. We're here to help you."

"What's your name?" asked Jake.

"David."

Landon and Jake's eyes both widened. Jake could barely recognize David and felt his heart pound with joy.

"Mrs. Gonzalez, the Principal, she's your mom, right?"

"Yeah," replied David weakly.

"And, your names are?" asked Landon.

"Susie and this is my sister, Megan," whispered one of two girls as Jake ran over and hugged them both.

"It's me, Jake! Don't worry ladies, I'm… er… we are going to get you home. I promise."

"Susie and Megan, this is Sweet Tooth and these are the Halloweenies, Anne and Lynn. David this is Frank, they will not let anyone or anything hurt you, okay? Stay together, stay quiet, and we'll get you out of here. Is there anyone else locked up down here?" whispered Landon.

"There were a lot of us. But…" Megan's voice trailed and her stare made Landon uneasy, like she had seen something more terrifying than words could ever describe.

"It killed themall. Ripped them apart. We're all that's left. I think it forgot about us," whispered Susie.

"We are getting you out of here, now. Let's go," ordered Landon.

Sweet Tooth, the Halloweenies, and Frank paired up with the children and helped them walk out of the dungeon and up to the ground level of Vyle's lair. Once they reached the ground level, Captain Bones began to take them on a different route than which they had come down from.

"Where are you going? Why aren't we going back the way we came?" Landon asked impatiently.

"We can't go that way to get out. Remember how we got in here in the first place? We have to go out the front," said Captain Bones.

"Mmhmn," said Jake to Landon with both eyes opened widely as though to say, "feels like a trap."

As they followed Captain Bones through the tower, they reached a room that had six enormous Nightmare statues standing in a circle staring down upon them with brightly burning green eyes of fire and black liquid pouring from their silver mouths into the black floor.

"Okay, that's just creepy!" Jake whispered.

"Where do we go now?" Jeckles asked Captain Bones, who had paused a moment gain his bearings.

"This way," whispered Captain Bones, pointing at two giant metal doors on the other side of the room.

"Help me push these open," whispered Captain Bones to Simon and the boys.

It took them a few tries to push the doors open, but after a few good shoulder slams, they cracked the doors open just enough to fit everyone through. There was a moment of panic as the group followed Captain Bones through the door into another dimly lit great room and found a Reaper floating in its center.

"Keep to the shadows and do not make a sound!" Captain Bones ordered.

Landon and Jake hid the light of their weapons as the group formed a tight line behind Captain Bones and crept along the walls, staying covered by the darkness. There was a moment when the Reaper twitched and faced their direction, but it did not move and they were able to continue their exit. With each step Landon took, he felt the air become thinner and cold, making it hard for him to breathe. Suddenly, the sleeping torches that lined the walls above them flickered on as they slowly crept under them, drawing the Reapers attention.

Landon placed his hand on the hilt of his blade, preparing to draw his sword when something behind the Reaper caught his eye. Something in the dark was coming towards them. Landon quickly unsheathed his sword and pointed the glowing blade towards it.

"What are you doing? It will see you!" said Jake frantically.

"There is something behind the Reaper," replied Landon.

Captain Bones took a few steps forward into the light, took out his sword and looked over his shoulder at the group. With a smile upon his face, he nodded his head and winked. Suddenly, the darkness roared and hundreds of tiny green flames flickered all around them. Jake looked at Landon and screamed,

"It's a trap!"

Chapter Twenty-Two: The Worst Nightmare…

Simon lunged at Captain Bones with purple fire blazing in both of his long hands but before Simon could reach him, Captain Bones was quickly wrapped in chains and violently wrenched into the darkness. The group readied their weapons as a horde of putrid Nightmares surrounded them.

A green fireball shot up over Landon's head, illuminating the dark room as it hovered above. Seated high upon a sinister throne, above the swarm of salivating Nightmares, sat Lord Vyle, King of the Nightmares. His crown of six blackened blades piercing through the pale skin of his skeletal face. Green fire danced wildly within the dark pits of his eye sockets as his long, silver teeth salivated and dripped. Vyle stood up from his throne, starring down at Landon he spoke in a voice that froze Landon's veins with fear.

"Hello, child."

Vyle gnashed his teeth and smiled, his blazing eyes locked with Landon's as he calmly descended the steps of his tortuous throne. With each step, Landon felt fear shorten his breath and grip his nerves. The Nightmares parted for their king and bowed as he slowly marched towards him, still staring. Vyle laughed wickedly; it sent shivers down his spine.

"Stay behind me," said Simon as he moved in front of Landon.

Simon quickly raised his burning fist and then threw a purple fireball directly at Vyle's terrifying face. The fireball swiftly cut through the frigid air and over the swarm of wicked Nightmares. Vyle did not stop walking as it rocketed towards him. Just before it hit his skeletal face, Vyle immediately caught the purple ball of fire, held it briefly in his silver clawed hand and then shoved the it into his mouth and smothered the flames by swallowing it. Then, Vyle

Landon searched the room, frantically looking for an escape as Vyle continued to make his way towards them. Then, he spotted it. Off in the distance, he could see a door. Landon closed his eyes, took in a deep breath, and then raised his sword high up over his head. He imagined the blade glowing brightly, but the sounds of the Nightmares teeth chattering made it hard to stay focused. With every step Vyle took Landon felt an anxiety building. He was afraid. His blood pumped vigorously and made his heart feel like it was going to burst, but he did not quit. He kept focusing and imagining.

Suddenly, a loud agonizing scream broke through the throne room. Landon opened his eyes and looked at his sword. It was glowing brightly. So brightly that the light obliterated the closest Nightmare. Jake immediately followed Landon actions, only now he had created a second hatchet that was helping to keep the Nightmares.

"That will not stop me, child," screamed Vyle.

Vyle and his Nightmares howled in horrible laughter. The sound of their gnashing teeth and laughter shook the walls of the throne room and made Mad Jack's hair puff up once more.

"I'm warning you," said Landon lifting his sword.

"Then, by all means, kill me!"

Landon nodded and even though he felt completely and utterly afraid, he walked towards his Nightmare. Simon grabbed his shoulder, but Landon shook his head and pushed his hand away, tapping his pocket.

As he walked through the wretched horde of Nightmares, the sounds of grinding teeth unnerved him and the putrid smell of rotting flesh nauseated him. With each step his muscles tightened and his heart beat wildly. Vyle looked as though he could smell his fear through the saturating drops of his sweat. Yet, Landon did not stop until he stood directly in front of his Nightmare.

Vyle stood directly in front of Landon, towering over him, his body glowing with red embers, his emerald eyes burning intensely as he snapped his teeth sinisterly and clicked his sharp silver claws, leaning down into Landon's face. Landon's heart beat even faster and harder. Fear didn't just take over his body, it suddenly held him hostage, making it almost impossible to move.

"Do you know who I am, child?" Vyle asked delightfully.

"Yes, I know what you are. You have haunted my dreams and tormented my dreams since the day we met. You are my Nightmare, Vyle," replied Landon, trying to stem his shaking voice.

"And, you are afraid."

"Yes. But, fear will not stop me."

"Child, you barely know the true feeling of fear, let alone its meaning… yet. Oh, I will show you such torturous wonders. I will tear you apart from the inside out and that will only be just the beginning."

Vyle laughed wickedly then raised his fist high above his head. The entire room fell silent. He stared right into Landon's eyes and whispered,

"Kill them all."

The Nightmares roared as they circled the group. Landon reached down into his pocket and pulled out the folded cloth. Vyle slashed his long silver claws down at Landon and sunk them into his shoulder, causing him to scream in agony and fall to his knees.

"Yes!" Vyle roared.

As Landon pulled the sparkling ring from the cloth, the stone's light began to beam. Shreak jumped from behind his king, grabbed at his hand, and shoved it back into the cloth as he tried to yank the stone from Landon's hand, screaming to Vyle,

"The Luminescent stone! Master, run!"

As they wrestled, Landon could feel the ring slide onto his finger. At that moment, Landon did not feel any fear. Instead, all he felt was rage. A rage that suddenly delivered a surge of light, tracing down the veins in his arm, into the ring, and then out of the stone directly toward Vyle.

Before the powerful light immediately destroyed Shreak, shredding the darkness and annihilating the Nightmares all around them, Vyle escaped the light, bursting into a giant cloud of smoke and ash that quickly disappeared into the rippling black floor.

The beaming light started to make Landon's arm shake as it surged with power and made it difficult to hold his arm steady. Just as his muscles began to hurt, the stone's powerful light quickly faded and Landon felt his arm return to normal.

"What happened?" Sweet Tooth asked nervously.

"I don't know. Maybe that's all the stone's got, Landon said, wrapping the ring back in the scarf and shoving back it into his pocket."

"Simon, over there!" yelled Jeckles, pointing to somebody lying on the ground in the corner of the room.

"Dozer!" yelled Simon.

The frail Sandman was badly beaten and had been chained to the dark Endindrium. Frank ran to the Sandman and smashed his giant boulder onto the chain links, breaking Dozer free from the dark Endindrium. Simon lifted the unresponsive Sandman and threw him into the Endindrium.

"Run!" shouted Jeckles as the floor started began to shake.

Vyle rose from the floor, his burning emerald eyes flickering, teeth grinding, and thick black smoke filling the room.

"Child!" he screamed as he raced towards Landon.

Landon dodged Vyle's attack, prompting the Halloweenies to throw candies that exploded like fireworks at him.

"Through the Endindrium," Simon shouted as he grabbed the Halloweenies and threw them into that dark passageway.

Landon and the group quickly followed and jumped into a swirling vortex. Vyle screamed angrily, smothering the fireworks, and dove in after them, slashing at Mad Jack's back leg and causing his whole body burn as they all fell into the dark portal.

Black clouds spiraled all around them as green flames threatened to burn their skin when suddenly, Landon felt his body crunch onto the cold surface of a dusty hard wooden floor.

"MOVE IT!" Jake shouted, pulling Landon up off the floor and pushing him out into what looked like a condemned house.

"Yeah, move it!" screamed Jeckles, pushing Jake down the stairs while everyone else followed.

They ran as fast as they could down a bunch of rickety stairs and burst through a broken wooden door out onto a dimly lit street.

"Is this my world?" Landon asked as they ran.

"I believe so," said Simon.

Suddenly, the streetlights behind them rapidly started to explode as they were smothered in black smoke. Landon saw the wild flicker of Vyle's emerald eyes as he savagely tore down the road after them.

"I know where we are. I KNOW WHERE WE ARE! This way," Jake screamed, darting towards a big yellow house, hopping over its fence, and landing face first onto the grass of the backyard.

Simon swooped up the Halloweenies and followed Landon and Jake as they jumped over fences and raced through several backyards with Vyle hot on their trail, smashing everything in his path.

Landon and the rest of the group helped Susie and Megan over the fence as Mad Jack jumped over all of them with Alexia and David on his back, landing their street, December Drive.

"Landon, your house is just up ahead!" Jake yelled as he reached for both of his hatchets, but they were gone.

Jake panicked and ran, but two steps into running, he tripped over a lawn chair that immediately triggered an automatic light sensor in Roger's backyard. The light cut into the darkness and buried itself into the swelling black smoke of Vyle that was pouring through the fance and reaching out to suffocate Jake.

The light burned through Vyle and made him retreat as he screamed in pain, leaving Jake behind as the king of Nightmares went to extinguish the light. Jeckles and Landon pulled Jake off the ground, took advantage of the moment, quickly ran into Landon's house.

"What are we going to do?" Sweet Tooth asked frantically.

Landon's mind drew a blank. He didn't know what he could do. They had no power in his world. Then, like lighting, an idea struck him.

"Simon! We have to get to Reflection City!" Landon ordered.

"What? Why?" Jake asked as he nervously locked the door behind him.

"Here in our world, Vyle gains power. In Nod, we have OUR power!" Landon hurriedly explained.

Jeckles popped open the top of his cane and pulled out a small silver ring with a single diamond stone and showed it to Landon and said,

"Take me to a mirror."

Landon and the group tore through the house searching for a mirror, but they wer all smashed. All except one.

"The attic!" yelled Landon.

Landon and the group ran up the stairs and pulled down the ladder to the attic just as Vyle ripped the door off the wall and poured into the house below.

"You're mine, you're all mine!" Vyle hissed.

Quickly they hurried up into the attic and ran over to the mirror. Jeckles put the ring on his finger and placed his hand onto the mirror's surface. Suddenly, the glass turned to liquid and rippled as each one of them jumped through it.

Vyle exploded up into the attic just as Simon and Jeckles jumped through the open portal. Before Jeckles could fully enter the mirror, Vyle grabbed his leg. Jeckles screamed in agony as his body burned. Simon reached back through the colorful portal and pulled Jeckles free from Vyle's clutches, kicking Vyle in his teeth.

As Simon pulled Jeckles into his chest, he watched his tiny eyes roll back and felt Jeckles body start to convulse while they all fell between worlds. He was changing.

Landon once again found his body falling through the Endindrium and then slam down onto the ground in the center of

Reflection City, outside The Fountain of Dreams. One by one they stood up and found themselves surrounded by Endindriums and Dreamers.

"Everybody get back!" hissed Mad Jack.

Simon and Jeckles fell through the Endindrium and landed right in front of Landon. Simon scrambled up to his feet and pushed Landon away from the Endindrium just as Vyle poured out into the Dreamer city, filling the sacred space with black smoke and ash and sending everyone into a frenzy.

All the strings of lights surrounding the city enraged Vyle as they burned his Nightmare body causing Vyle to wrap himself in a spinning cocoon of smoke and ash. Then, like a bomb, he sent waves of smoke out over the city.

They smothered the lights and blanketed the surrounding city in darkness. As the city dimmed, Vyle rose from the ground and stood before the city. He reached out for Landon, but before he could snare him, Simon leapt in front of him. Vyle dug his claws into Simon and hissed as he twisted them into his body.

"This time, I will finish what I started!" screamed Vyle.

Simon felt his body burning inside as Vyle poured a thick black smoke into him.

"R… un," Simon whispered as Vyle sank his claws deeper and he fell limp onto his knees.

"NO!" screamed Landon angrily.

Landon reached back into his pocket to retrieve the Luminescent stone but it was gone. His heart fluttered, and he began to panic. Vyle laughed wickedly as he slashed at Simon's chest. Jake conjured up his hatchets and attacked Vyle, but the Nightmare King effortlessly tossed him away.

Landon looked all around him at the group and the surrounding Dreamers. He saw terror and fear fill their eyes. The whole city was frozen in panic. Landon closed his eyes and desperately tried to focus, but fear clouded his mind. He had to calm down. Landon opened his eyes and started taking in deep breaths. Once more, time slowed to a crawl.

Letting the air loose from his lungs, Landon closed his eyes, cleared his mind, and let his mind wander. He pictured the city and then Simon under Vyle's grip. The city and everyone around him became engulfed in darkness, all except for Simon.

Within Landon's mind's eye, the bandages wrapped around Simon's face slowly unraveled. Layer upon layer the bandages fell until they exposed what was hidden underneath. Where Simon's face should be, was a black hole.

As Landon stared into the black hole, his hand felt warm. From the corner of his eye Landon could see something glowing. He held his hand up and watched as it radiated a brilliant white light, just like that of the Luminescent Stone. He looked over at Simon and then reached his beaming hand into a black hole. The brilliant light poured into the black hole and into Simon. Landon opened his eyes, they were glowing white.

"What is this?" hissed Vyle as he retreated from the light starting to beam brighter.

Together, Landon and Simon began to float and as they did, Landon reached out and touched Simon's bandaged forehead. Simon's entire body suddenly beamed so bright he had become even brighter than the light of the Luminescent stone.

Vyle screamed defiantly as his body ripped apart under the brilliant white light. He had nowhere to hide. His entire body twisting and turning as he was slammed against the elegant silver frame of the Endindrium they came out of.

"You will never harm another child or Dreamer ever again!" screamed Landon and Simon simultaneously.

As they floated higher into the air, Simon's light began to pulse and destroy the blankets of smoke and ash over the entire city. The light pouring from Simon's body destroyed every single shadow in Reflection City. With one last pulse, Vyle's body exploded into pieces and disintegrated in the beautiful white light.

Simon and Landon floated back to the ground and the light that beamed so brightly from Simon's body and Landon's eyes, dimmed.

"There!" screamed Sweet Tooth, pointing at a single wisp of black smoke climbing up the base of the Endindrium.

But, before anyone could catch the tiny wisp of smoke that was left of Vyle, dove into the Endindrium and disappeared.

"It's not over…" Landon whispered.

Once more, he took in a deep breath, closed his eyes, and created a new sword. He then approached the Endindrium and stabbed the glowing blade right into its center. The glass exploded, raining its shattered pieces over him, and cutting small slices into his face, dissolving into a fine white sand as it fell to the ground.

Landon turned around and suddenly, all at once, the crowd of Dreamers erupted into a roaring applause and cheered all around the group. As the crowd excitedly rushed them, Simon reached down and picked up Jeckles from the ground and carried him over to the group.

"I'm… I'm… just like you." Jeckles whispered in an eerie voice.

Jeckles was no longer smooth. He had become fuzzy and had two fangs that stuck up from his bottom lip, out of his mouth. With a coughing chuckle and a smile flickering within the flames of his blue burning eyes. Jeckles looked up at Simon, holding up his hands and showing Simon the silver claws piercing through his white gloves, he said,

"Now, you're not the only one."

Chapter Twenty-Three: A Child's Request...

Warm golden rays of the sun stretched up and over the land of Nod onto the streets and Dreamers of Reflection City. Landon felt the sun touch his skin as he nursed a throbbing headache by rubbing his temples. He closed his eyes and breathed in deeply as a gentle calm washed over him and the pain subsided.

Dreamers large and small, tall and short, flying and walking, all gathered around the group at the center of Reflection City and applauded so vigorously that Landon could feel the ground tremble under his feet. Simon raised Jeckles over his head so he could see the cheering crowd and watched Jeckles smile a sharp, toothy grin.

Not a single Dreamer had any fear of Simon or Jeckles. In fact, the entire city smiled upon them both as they rejoiced which made Simon's heart feel a magnificent joy he had not felt since the first day he met Landon.

"We did it," said Jake, smiling over at Landon.

Landon smiled back, yet, he couldn't help but wonder what happened to the little wisp of smoke that was Vyle after he escaped through the Endindrium. However, this wonder disappeared when his eyes locked with Alexia's.

Landon and Jake walked over to Alexia, helped her down off of Mad Jack's back, and then joyfully embraced in a comforting hug. Suddenly, the crowd became silent. Landon turned and saw a soft golden light hovering above their heads gently descending towards them.

The surrounding Dreamers bowed as the golden light floated down into the city. Simon however, did not bow. In fact, he stood up as straight and as tall as he possibly could while stopping the rest of the group from bowing as well.

The golden light dimmed and Landon could see it was coming from a tiny crystal floating less than an inch away from the muscular chest of an enormous man. Surrounding him with golden light were several rings hypnotically circling around his massive frame.

He wore a long flowing white and gold trimmed cloak that waved gracefully in the wind, flowing out from underneath his gleaming golden armor that glittered under the sun as he stood before the group.

In his mighty hand, the giant man held a long staff made of a deep red wood. There were several jewels and precious metals with intricately carved symbols all around it. Hovering proudly, just above the tip of the staff, was a floating crystal sphere. Within the sphere, swirling around within, were beautiful golden granules of sand. As Landon turned his sight from the sand, he was drawn into the man's soft glowing yellow eyes that stared down upon him from underneath the hood of his cloak. His tan skin sparkled with golden flakes and he seemed to radiate warmth as he approached the frail Sandman and knelt down next to him.

He reached down and gently lifted Dozer up into the palm of his enormous hand. Then, he softly spoke a language Landon and the other children had never heard. The golden sand within the sphere swirled faster until it glowed. Then a golden light wrapped around the frail Sandman's body and then gently lifted Dozer's body up into the air above the man's gigantic palm. The entire city remained silent as they witnessed the broken Sandman's body heal.

First, Dozer's cloak and armor were magically cleaned and looked very similar this giant man. Next, the gray in Dozer's eyes cleared and became vibrantly yellow. And finally, his pale and aged skin quickly bronzed while the gray of his hair transformed into sparkling strands of long, thick, brown curls.

As the light faded, Dozer stood smiling and glowing upon the massive palm, his wounds healed. He then lowered his head and dropped to one knee.

"Thank you," said Dozer with a much stronger voice.

"You are welcome."

Dozer was set down and the Dreamers of the group quickly gathered around him. They hugged him and welcoming him back. Then, Dozer turned and once again knelt down onto a single knee.

"My magic was used to make a cursed Endindrium. I tried... to hold out for as long as I could, but..." said Dozer shamefully as he lowered his head.

The giant man gently touched Dozer's shoulder and then with one huge finger he reached under Dozer's chin and lifted his head up.

"I am here," said Dozer's master.

The giant man closed his brilliant eyes and then shrank his body from its enormous size to that of the height of Dozer. The golden man then placed both of his hands upon Dozer's shoulders, took in a deep breath, and softly exhaled a white mist that quickly absorbed into Dozer's body. Once the mist was absorbed, it exploded into a dazzling blue light underneath the surface of his bronze skin and traced through the highways of his veins like colorful lightning.

Then, he removed his hands from Dozer and smiled. The blue light raced up into his heart and made his chest beam a magical golden light that became so bright the two of them disappeared within its radiance. In a flash that magnificent light shot up into the sky and exploded over the city like fireworks that trickled down like a beautiful glowing rain. Then, Landon and the city watched as the man descended alone.

"Where did you send him?" Simon asked, sounding irritated.

The golden man turned to Simon. He gently lifted his strong hands and removed his hood. His smooth bald head gleamed from the golden rays of light swirling around him. His eyes glowing brightly. He stared at Simon for a moment, smiled, and then replied,

"Dozer is a Sandman. He must answer to Deity. For now, only she can guide him."

Suddenly, the Dreamers surrounding the group parted as seven silver Dreamers floated gracefully towards them. The seven beautiful Dreamers, draped in shimmering silver robes, briefly lowered their heads robes as they floated past and made their way to Landon and Simon.

Landon could see that three of the silver Dreamers were female and three were male. The leading silver Dreamer was neither male nor female. Instead, this being was constanly rippling.

Then, like a heavenly chorus, they all spoke together at once in a beautiful harmony that resonated right into the deepest part of Landon's being,

"Welcome."

Landon and the other children were captivated by their big crystal blue eyes and found it difficult to look away. Their bodies shimmered like the ocean at sunrise and upon their heads were pearl white crowns, with onyx stones and elegant symbols carved into them. In fact, Landon noticed right away that those symbols looked much like the ones that were carved into the bone of Death's Hand under the Bosque De Los Muertos.

The rippling Dreamer reached out and took the golden man by his hand then stood quietly, staring at each other for a moment until the man bowed once more.

"My name is Mada Ra," said the Sandman with a deep bow and a kind voice. "I am a creation of Neith and child of Rasdem. I am happy to meet you. Sentinel would like to speak with you and Simon."

Once Landon and Simon agreed, the silver Dreamers formed a circle around Landon and Simon which spun around them faster and faster. Suddenly, the city disappeared and everyone else as a silver sphere engulfed them. All of a sudden, the sphere faded and both Landon and Simon became weightless. They were floating in space.

Surrounded by glittering stars, colorful planets, and diamond wakes from the tails of fiery comets soaring through oceans of neon gas clusters and clouds all floating in the beauty of the cosmos, Sentinel floated with Landon and Simon. They were sitting in a circle around them with their legs crossed and hands resting upon their knees.

"We are Sentinel. We seven are one. No more and no less. We were woven into this existence by the dreaming threads of the Root. We are beings of harmony, and guardians of The Vein," they sang beautifully as the rippling Dreamer moved towards them. "You child, you have question. Simply ask."

Landon took a moment, stared down onto a sparkling galaxy slowly spinning in the cosmos below his feet. And, after a lengthy moment of silence, he asked,

"How can Simon change back into the Dreamer he once was?"

Staring below, a beautiful explosion of colors Landon had never seen before, birthed from the blooming nebulae, creating a galaxy as though it were the cue for Sentinel to respond.

"That which exists, is ever bound to the dreaming threads of the Root. These threads are woven deeply into the fabric of the universe. Tempered by conflict and resolution. We do not know of a way to restore Simon back to the Dreamer he once was, but that does not mean there isn't a possibility."

The rippling Dreamer slowly drifted closer to Landon and Simon, then lightly placed both hands upon their chests. Landon instantly felt his body warm and his wounds healed. The touch sent rippling blue streams of reflecting light across their bodies as though they were underwater, making them feel completely at ease and calm. Then, the silver Dreamer pulled back and returned to the circle.

"Landon, your heart hurts. You worry that when you return to your world, you will never see Simon nor any other Dreamer and Nod ever again." they sang in a deep sorrowful melody.

Sentinel lifted their arms and joined hands. Suddenly, stars burst like fireworks as meteors rocketed in and out of their circle. Sentinel changed colors and as they did, their bodies pulsed with bolts of electricity like a storming sky. The three male Dreamers turned from silver to red and the three female Dreamers had turned from silver to blue.

"Simon, hold out your ring." they sang.

Simon reached into his pocket and withdrew the ring he had showed Landon when he first came to Nod. As the ring and its black stone lay in the center of his long palm, Simon and Landon watched it float up and start to spin. A soft chorus of bells chimed an enchanting melody as several tiny shooting stars raced through its center, making it spin even faster. One of the shooting stars flew by Landon's face and when it did, he saw it was actually a tiny crystal fairy with diamond dust trailing her wake like a like comet.

A small red glowing orb fell down from above their heads, hovering briefly before gently setting down upon the ring's black stone. The stone instantly absorbed the orb and melted the balck away, transforming the stone into a beautiful diamond. The ring then slowed and came to a stop as it floated back down into Simon's palm.

"You truly are a beautiful Dreamer." they sang.

"Dreamer?" asked Simon confused.

"Sentinel recognizes a Dreamer's heart and you Simon, are a Dreamer." sang Sentinel beautifully.

Landon could not see behind Simon's bandaged face, but he sensed that Simon was smiling. Sentinel then lifted their hands and pointed their fingers at Landon.

"You can Pretend," sang Sentinel as Landon nodded in agreement, reaching up and touching his head.

"Yes," answered Landon.

"This is makes you dangerous and why you and your kind are forbidden to ever return to Nod. A child's ability to pretend, especially one as powerful as yours, can destroy everything we are. Sentinel, must protect Nod. This is why you and the rest of the children may never return."

"If you do, the consequences will be grave. As a parting gift, we recognize not only Simon but, Jeckles, Frank, Anne, Lynn, Anastasia, Sweet Tooth and Mad Jack as Dreamers that have connected with you and the other children. Therefore, it is our decision that they may continue to share in each of your lives until you reach the age of thirteen," Sentinel warned eerily.

Suddenly, the stars all around them twinkled brightly and bathe Sentinel in a dazzling spectrum of colorful lights that blinded both Landon and Simon. When their vision cleared, they once again stood back in the center of Reflection City.

"You am again Dreambir!" yelled Frank, crushing Simon as he wrapped his powerful arms around his body in a bear hug and squeezed him so hard that it Simon lost his breath.

"You could see us?" Landon asked the group.

"No, but Mada could and he pretty much gave us a play-by-play." replied Jake. "Man, that guy can see everything! Did you know that he knows where I live and..."

"And that you sleep with is a stuffed..." Sweet Tooth tried to say, but was immediately muffled after Jake threw his hands over his little mouth and shouted with a cracking voice,

"PILLOW!"

Jake quickly cleared his throat and nervously shifted his big eyes around while obnoxiously coughing and blaming the cracking of his voice on all the smoke he had breathed in from Vyle.

"Hey, check it out!" said Jake, excited to switch topics as he pointed to Alexia and the other children who had been healed.

"You guys are all back to normal! How do you feel?" Landon asked eagerly.

"Much better, what about you guys?" Alexia asked the three other children who all smiled and agreed.

"Who healed you? Was it Sentinel?" Landon questioned.

"No, it was Mada. He healed us while you were gone. It was amazing!" David answered happily.

"Landon! Look," said Simon excitedly, holding out his ring and showing him that the stone had become crystal clear.

"I... I can come see you now," said Simon as he placed the ring on his finger.

"That is if you want me to."

"Of course, I do," Landon replied happily.

Mada approached Landon and briefly bowed his head before whispering into his ear and asking,

"Do you still have the Luminescent Stone?"

"No, I lost it," Landon replied as he pulled out his pocket to show them the hole.

Mada smiled and bowed once more, then turned away, and in a ray of golden light, disappeared up into the sunlight. Landon took a moment and looked out upon Reflection City. He wanted to get a good look at it before they left. Many of the city's lights had been destroyed from their battle with Vyle and shadows now darkened more of their city.

Landon looked over at the cheering Dreamers and then back over at the shadows. As he stared into the darkness, flashes of lurking Nightmares ran through his mind. How could he leave this place with no protection after bringing Vyle to Reflection City? What if the Nightmares came looking for their master? These questions weighed heavily on Landon. And then, he had a moment of clarity.

Landon closed his eyes and let his let his mind drift. He fell into his mind's eye and landed within the labyrinth of his imagination. As he wandered through the blank canvas of his mind, Reflection City began to form all around.

Landon quickly found himself walking into the shadows of a dark alley between two sleeping buildings. A cool breeze wrapped around him as he came to a stop and quietly stood in the dark alley. He stared into the shadows, looking for movement, but they were empty.

Suddenly, Landon's head became heavy, making him look down at the ground beneath him. There was something small wrapped in black cloth laying between his feet. Landon bent over, reached down, and slowly pulled the cloth away. Instantly, he felt warm as the darkness completely disappeared. In his hand, Landon held a brilliant orb burning with a beautiful silver and white fire that licked at his hands but did not burn him.

The sudden sounds of awe pulled Landon out from his mind's eye. He did not immediately open his eyes, instead he braced for the searing pain to fill his head. But this time, it didn't.

Rather than feeling pain, a wonderful and soothing warmth filled both of his hands. Then, Landon slowly opened his eyes and saw the silver light from a burning orb resting within the palms of his hands. It did not blind him nor anyone else. He smiled and then handed the orb over to a nearby bald, solid black, Dreamer with colorful wings made of floating shards of glowing glass.

"What is your name?" he asked.

"Maynard," the Dreamer nasally answered.

"Are you kidding me?" Landon sighed, looking over and seeing Jake's eyes widen with delight.

"New favorite Dreamer right there! shouted Jake, shooting a wink and finger guns at Maynard.

"Hey!" shouted Jeckles, flipping his middle finger up at Jake.

"Can you put this somewhere that it can shine over the whole city?" Landon asked.

"I know the perfect place for it," Maynard replied, graciously accepting the orb and then flew up into the sky towards the Fountain of Dreams.

"Nicely done, amigo," said Jake as the two boys bumped the sides of their fists together.

Maynard flew high up into the pastel sky and then completely disappeared from sight. She flew right up to the tip top of the Fountain of Dreams and landed down upon a small circular platform surrounded by the beautiful water that flowed down to the Endindriums. She then reached into a small red pouch on the side of her hip and sprinkled a handful of silver glitter onto the platform that formed into a glittering pillar to place the bright orb upon. She then secured the beaming ball of light orb and watched as it poured over all of Reflection City.

And, just like in Landon's mind, the darkness disappeared throughout the entire Dreamer city as it beautifully bathed in the orb's warm silver light. The Dreamers cheered and thanked Landon and the group for saving their city. Even the buildings showed their thanks by standing still and up tall. Allowing the Dreamers inside to come out and cheer along with the crowd. Landon enjoyed the feeling for a moment. but knew he and the others had to leave.

"Well, I guess it's time for us to go home..." Landon said to Simon.

Simon nodded and then approached an Endindrium. As he lifted his hand with the ring on it, Simon paused for a moment to admire the sparkling diamond, and then reached out and touched the reflective surface of the Endindrium. His long fingers disappeared into the rippling mirror and Simon's heart filled with immense joy.

"After you," said Simon happily.

As Landon and the rest of the children made their way to the Endindrium, Landon turned back to the group of Dreamers, smiled and asked,

"See you soon?"

"Soon me see you too!" Frank shouted excitedly as he accidentally tossed his giant boulder onto a nearby group of tiny Dreamers that ended up running away with the big rock.

Landon and the children said their goodbyes and then, one by one, they disappeared through the magical Endindrium, and left the land of Nod. As the city of Dreamers waved goodbye and rejoiced, one of Reflection City's residents had stayed out of sight and away from the crowd.

Stilts, shrouded in his deep red cloak and drawing no attention to himself, slowly made his way to the shattered Endindrium that Vyle had escaped through, knelt down and saw a piece of dark cloth lying under the frame of the shattered Endindrium. He quickly reached his crystal hand out and picked up the cloth.

Overlooked by the crowd, Stilts quickly made his way to a close by garden and hid within its thick foliage. He then held up his crystal hand, unfolded the cloth, and saw the black bone ring of the Luminescent Stone resting in his palm. From under his hood, he smiled, starring down into the stone and watching a tiny flicker of light dancing inside. Then, he quickly covered the ring, carefully placed it inside of his cloak, and disappeared back into the city.

Chapter Twenty-Four: Who is Dreaming...

One by one, the children stepped out from the mirror and into Landon's attic, making their way down into the living room. The house had been cleaned, so Landon knew his parents had been home, but they were nowhere to be found.

"I wonder where my parents are?" said Landon.

"Maybe they are at my house," replied Jake.

"Yeah, maybe. What are we going to tell them?"

"I don't even know, man..." Jake answered, with a confused look on his face. "But, what I do know is that my parents are going to definitely call the cops and everyone is going to want some details, especially, like, how we got away," Jake warned.

"Well, we can't just go in there and tell them about the Nightmares and Nod. We need a believable story," said Landon.

The children stood quietly for a moment, each one thinking.

Suddenly, a loud thumping came from upstairs and made everyone jump, including Simon how hit his head on the ceiling. The thumping grew louder as it ran down the stairs towards them. Landon grabbed for his sword but it was gone. He and the others looked at each other and braced for whatever was barreling down towards the living room. Then, jumping out from the darkness, Jangers leapt up onto Landon's chest, knocked him down, and excitedly started licking his face.

"Jangers!" Landon screamed enthusiastically.

After celebrating with Jangers for a moment, Landon then returned to figure out a believable story with the group of children.

"Alright, how about this. We were kidnapped. And... it was very dark," said David.

"Yeah and what if the kidnappers got scared? So, they dropped us off at the old Conroy Park... and just left," said Jake.

"And, what if we say we were all blindfolded..." added Susie.

"Yeah, that is a great idea. We can say that we came to your house first because it's the closest to the park! Other than that, we have no clue who they were or where we were at," Jake concluded.

"Like we had been kept in a dark room? Like we were chained up and couldn't see?" asked Megan rhetorically.

"It's okay, we are safe now. It's over. Right?" whispered Susie as she attempted to comfort Megan.

"Is it?" Megan replied angrily.

"Maybe it isn't. At least we know how to kill Nightmares if they ever come after us again. But, for now... we have to have a story that our parents will believe," said Landon.

"And what about Roger?" Alexia asked.

"Oh yeah..." whispered Jake solemnly. "I think we should tell his parents he... that he died."

"How do we do that?" asked David.

"I'll tell them. After all... I saw him die," Alexia answered as tears streamed down her cheeks.

Simon reached over and pulled Alexia into his arms. The rest of the group followed and hugged Alexia. Together they agreed not just on their story, but to always be there for each other. Then, after wiping away the tears and collecting themselves, they rehearsed their story several times before leaving to Jake's house. But, before they left, Landon turned to Simon and pulled him to the side and asked,

"You should probably go, huh?"

"Yes," Simon replied.

"See you later?"

"See you later," Simon nodded, then reached out, pulled Landon into a hug before walking up the stairs and disappearing into the attic where he then entered the mirror and returned to Nod.

Landon left his house with the others and headed next door with the rest of the children. Jake's mother, Wanda Jackson, had been sitting at the kitchen table, staring blankly down at the floor with her hands holding up her head when she heard Jake's voice burst through the front door.

"Mom! Dad!" Jake shouted.

"Jake? Jake! JAKE! Idris, it's Jake!" screamed his mother.

Wanda frantically sprang up from the chair and sprinted to the front door. She was a tall and curvy woman with long twisting black. Her face drenched with tears as she wrapped her arms tightly around him.

"Son?" shouted a voice from above.

Jake's father, a handsome man with captivating eyes, raced down the stairs and quickly joined in the tight embrace. After several questions and the gathering of blankets to cover all the children, Idris called the police and then each of the children's parents.

As the police and parents arrived, Landon waited for his to come. One of the officers on the scene, talking to Jake's parents, pointed over to Landon, capturing his attention. Wanda and Idris looked very sad while the police officer's face seemed to fall with deep concern. Landon approached the officer and asked,

"Excuse me, have you seen my parents?"

Wanda burst into tears and then pulled him into her arms.

"Oh sweetheart!" she cried.

She started to sob so much that she could not speak. Idris pulled him away and then sat Landon down on a nearby couch in their living room. With sorrowful eyes, he told Landon what the officer had just told him.

"I'm sorry, son. The police just told me... us... your parents, they were in a car accident on their way here. They're alive, but unconscious. They are on the way to the hospital now," Idris said softly.

Landon felt his stomach clench, and the room started to spin. He immediately felt distant. The surrounding sounds muffled, Landon's body became numb, and the world fell into a blur.

"I think he's in shock. Son, can you hear me?" said a muffled voice.

"My name is Officer Frank Moreno. I am here with your uncle and we are going to take you to see your parents, okay?"

Landon barely acknowledged the police officer and then felt a large hand reach out and grab hold of his shoulder. It was a strong hand with a gentle grip that conjured him out of the distance.

"Hey buddy," said a warm familiar voice.

Landon traced the strong hand up to a tall man with long brown hair that he tucked behind his ears and draped his broad shoulders. He was wearing a red and white flannel shirt, beat up jeans, and boots. Landon looked up into his uncle's soft eyes looking down at him. Landon had always liked Jared's eyes because they never really stayed the same color and there was a twinkle of kindness in them that eased him.

"Uncle Jared?"

"Don't you worry, we are going to figure this all out," said Jared reassuringly.

Landon quickly retreated to the fog of his mind, back to where the world was muffled, as Jared turned and continued to talk to Officer Moreno. Eventually, he was placed in the back of Officer Moreno's patrol car along with his uncle and driven to the hospital.

When they arrived, the three of them quickly made their way to the third floor where Landon's parents were being treated. At the end of a long hallway, annoyingly humming with the buzz of white florescent lights, Landon ran down the room with his parents, looked in through a window in the wall and saw them both laying upon hospital beds, each one with a breathing apparatus attached to their face and wires running from their bodies into beeping monitors.

Officer Moreno opened the door for Jared and Landon to enter and then stepped back out into the hall, leaving them alone with Landon's parents.

"I'm so sorry, kiddo," said Jared, as he placed his hand on Landon's shoulder.

Jared crossed in front of Landon and knelt down. He then reached into his pocket and pulled out a folded piece of paper.

"This letter… this letter is going to tell you something that you may not fully understand. But, I made a promise to your father," said Jared softly.

"A letter?" Landon asked.

Jared sighed, then stood up and with the look of a saddened puppy dog, he placed the folded paper into Landon's hand and whispered,

"Everything you know about who you are is about to change and I am so sorry."

Confused, Landon wiped his eyes, unfolded the paper, and then began to read.

"Dearest Landon,

If you are reading this letter, you are in grave danger. What I am about to tell you may be hard to accept. As much as it pains me to write and admit, Moira and I are not your true birth parents. We were chosen to protect you and raise you as our own. From the very moment you were brought you to us, Moira and I have loved you as our own and we always will. You are truly magical. You always have been. And now, you are going to have to

find out just how magical you really are. Trust Jared and do

exactly what he says. Your life depends on it.

We love you more than you could ever know.

Love, Jensen and Moira

Landon's eyes filled with tears and his heart filled with an anger that made his blood boil as he threw the letter on the tile floor.

"Is this some kind of joke? This letter says they're not my real parents! What is this bullshit?"

Jared knelt down, wrapped his arms around Landon, and hugged him. Landon tucked his head into his shoulder and screamed. As he cried, Landon asked,

"Are they really not my parents?"

"Landon, those two over there raised you, love you, and have done everything to protect you. To me, that makes them your parents. I… " Jared answered before being interrupted by officer

Moreno knocking on the door and then requesting Jared's presence into the hall.

"I will be right back, okay?" Jared asked.

Landon let go of his uncle and nodded for him to go out into the hall. Once he was alone, he wiped the remaining tears from his eyes and then walked over to the gap between both of the hospital beds. He slowly traced his fingers over each of his parent's hands and watched as they both breathed through tubes, motionless. With a heavy heart, Landon turned and folded into a chair where he sat silently staring at his parents for almost half an hour.

Suddenly, a loud shuffling noise came from behind him and broke the silence. Landon quickly turned around and looked behind him, but nothing was there. The florescent lights in the room hummed loudly and began to flicker. Landon looked outside the window of the room into the hallway of the hospital and saw Officer Moreno and Jared were still talking and unaware of the flickering lights. He quickly pushed up off the chair and slowly approached his parents.

Another shuffling noise came from behind him along with a faint sound of chains clanking. Landon turned around again and still there was nothing there. All of the sudden, the hospital room became freezing cold and the lights shut off. At that moment Landon could hear something breathing behind him. He slowly turned around and saw two green eyes staring at him from the dark.

"Vyle!"

The emergency lights flicked on and the wisp of smoke that was Vyle shot right past him and then hovered directly above his parents. A wicked laugh shook the room and knocked Landon to the ground. Jared saw the emergency lights flash on, turned and looked into the room to find Landon laying on the floor. He tried to open the door, but it was stuck.

"Landon!" he screamed, pounding on the door.

"They're mine!" screamed Vyle.

Suddenly, time slowed to a crawl. Vyle screamed and sent a shock wave of smoke through the room that blew out the windows, lights and everything that could be shattered. As the shockwave sent Landon flying towards the wall, he felt tiny pieces of glass slowly slice through the skin on his arms as he raised them to cover his face.

Flying backwards through the cutting shards of glass and sparks of floating fire raining down over his head, Landon watched as both of his parents exploded into black glittering sand. Then, time suddenly sped back up and he smashed head first into the wall.

Jared and Officer Moreno kicked open the door just as the tiny wisp of black smoke slipped into the air vent of the hospital room. Landon's ears were ringing loudly as he fought to stay conscious. Through the piercing sound and blurring vision, he could faintly hear Vyle's wicked laughter echo through the vent as he escaped into the hospital. As his vision blackend, Landon whispered,

"Simon..."

Vyle traveled through the maze of hospital air ducts until he breached the building walls. From there he made his way, under the pale moonlight, down into the city. Racing between tall buildings and busy streets, all the way down into the sleeping neighborhood of Conroy Cove.

A few blocks from Landon's house, the tiny wisp of Vyle soared over the rooftops of Conroy cove, past the old Conroy park, and down onto a dimly lit road that led to a boarded-up house.

Vyle poured himself in-between the boards of the front door and into the dilapidated house, drifted up the stairs and into a room at the end of a narrow hallway. Standing in center of the room was the dark Endindrium that brought Vyle from Nyx.

The instant Vyle dove into the the Endindrium's rippling surface, the glass froze. The dark Endindrium shook violently, cracking the frozen glass, and then, like an erupting volcano, it exploded, sending pieces of shattered glass and ice throughout the room.

Dozer's magic reached its limit and transformed that dark Endindrium into a trap. A trap, that led directly to a place hidden within the darkest pit of the universe. Vyle was now trapped in the most abysmal and demonic hell in all existence, the sadistic and malevolent void of Euval.

To be continued...

Original 'Simon Hush' drawing

by Joshua Thomas Bray

15 December 2001